63615

F

W9-CBD-290

THE
TRAP

OTHER DELL YEARLING BOOKS YOU WILL ENJOY

DELL YEARLING BOOKS are designed especially to entertain and enlighten young people. Patricia Reilly Giff, consultant to this series, received her bachelor's degree from Marymount College and a master's degree in history from St. John's University. She holds a Professional Diploma in Reading and a Doctorate of Humane Letters from Hofstra University. She was a teacher and reading consultant for many years, and is the author of numerous books for young readers.

THE TRAP

JOAN LOWERY NIXON

A DELL YEARLING BOOK

Published by
Dell Yearling
an imprint of
Random House Children's Books
a division of Random House, Inc.
New York

Visit us on the Web! www.randomhouse.com/kids

Educators and librarians, for a variety of teaching tools, visit us at
www.randomhouse.com/teachers

ISBN: 0-440-22870-0

Reprinted by arrangement with Delacorte Press

Printed in the United States of America

May 2004

10 9 8 7 6 5 4 3 2 1

OPM

With love to the Hutchisons
Joy, Les, Susan, and Robert

Chapter One

I HAD NEVER BEEN ON A ROAD SO DARK AND LONELY. THE car's headlights drilled through a deep tunnel, illuminating only the pavement ahead. Trees and scrub that lined the roadside shifted into grotesque black shapes, looming, hovering, then disappearing into the night.

My father's aunt, Glenda Hollister, leaned forward, gripping the steering wheel. Without taking her gaze from the road, she said, "I didn't think to tell your father that I've got a bit of night blindness."

I stiffened in my seat. "You can't see where you're going?"

"Oh, it's not that bad," she scoffed, but she squinted, straining to see ahead, so I didn't believe her and stared at the road myself, as if there were something I could do.

"I just meant that it would have been easier if your plane had come in during the day," she added. "At best, Rancho del Oro is a good two-hour drive from the San Antonio airport."

We were spotlighted in a sudden yellow glare as a car came up behind us, then zipped past. For the first time I was glad that Aunt Glenda wasn't driving very fast, because she swerved, bumping along the gravel edges of the road, then steered back into the right lane. "I have a license. Why don't I drive?" I asked.

"It's sweet of you to offer, Julie," she said, "but you don't know the way. Now that we've passed Kerrville, the entrance to the ranch isn't far, and finding it is tricky."

She suddenly hit the brakes, and I braced myself against the dashboard. My heart pounding, I managed to gasp, "What happened?"

"This darned entrance," Aunt Glenda snapped. "I almost missed it myself." Without even a glance into the rearview mirror, she backed up about twenty feet, then swung out in a wide arc to face a barred gate that was fastened between two brick pillars, set back within a grove of mesquite trees. Over the gate was a rustic, dimly lit arch with the words RANCHO DEL ORO burned into the wood. Beyond lay an even narrower road, fading into a dark hole. Aunt Glenda pressed a button on a device that was fastened to the sun shield on the driver's side, and the gates opened, slowly and silently swinging apart.

"Almost home," she said wearily as the car bumped and shuddered over the boards of a cattle guard. "We're on El Camino Vista. It's a little winding, but it will take us right up the hill to our house."

I tried to see what we were passing, but I couldn't. There was a heavy cloud cover, and it was much too dark. "Where are the streetlights?" I asked.

She gave me a quick look. "You're a city girl, Julie. There are no streetlights on Texas ranches."

I couldn't help shivering. Barred gates, a night as black as a puddle of tar spread over a pothole, not a streetlight in sight—what in the world was I doing here?

Yesterday my father had said in his firmest voice, "We're counting on you, Julie. You're the only one who can help."

As he spoke Mom kept nodding, which flipped the turned-up ends of her short, dark brown hair, cut so much like mine. I know she was trying to emphasize the importance of what Dad was saying, but I wasn't in the mood to hear their point of view. And it didn't help that my younger sister and brothers, Bitsy, Hayden, and Trevor, were watching from the doorway—Trevor with a big grin on his face. I was furious. "You're telling me I have to give up the swim team?"

"It's not that we don't think the swim team is important," Mom said. Then her cheeks grew pink and I knew she was embarrassed as she added, "I mean, you don't have Olympic goals or great plans like that. It's just a swim team, so we all feel it's expendable, Julie. I hope you understand."

"The swim team is more important than you think," I told her. I tried not to ruin my argument with tears, and it was difficult to do. "Everyone on our team has worked hard, and this year, for the first time, we have a chance to make the Interstate Sweepstakes!"

"Please be reasonable." Mom was not quite begging. "I'm working on one of the biggest legal cases of my entire career. And your father has promised to lead that six-week seminar at UCLA. There's no way either of us can spend the summer with Aunt Glenda and Uncle Gabe."

I tried to keep my temper. I was not only angry, I was hurt because they didn't think what I wanted to do was important. "Why me?" I demanded of Dad. "Why should I spend the whole summer with *your* aunt and uncle? I hardly know them. I haven't seen them since they came to your family reunion four years ago. Why can't your brothers or your sister go?"

Dad shook his head, then stared down at his toes. I couldn't help noticing how the little bald spot on top of his head reflected the lamplight, and for just an instant I felt a strange jolt of sorrow, as if part of Dad were slowly slipping away.

"We discussed this problem thoroughly," he explained. "Ellen's going to be a grandmother any day now and has to be on hand to help Shelley with her twins. George and Samantha are leaving in two days for Europe, chaperoning George's high school choral group. And Richard is recovering from bypass surgery." He let out a long breath and went on. "It's just awful timing for everyone. So no arguments, Julie. The family thought it over and made the only decision we could make. You're the one family member who's available to stay with Aunt Glenda and help out when Uncle Gabe gets released from the hospital."

"Couldn't they get a nurse? She'd be more help to someone with a broken ankle than I would. It's not life or death. It's just an ankle!"

"Aunt Glenda wanted someone in the family to

come," Dad explained. "As a matter of fact, she insisted on family. When I spoke to her, she actually sounded a little shaken, a little frightened. She needs someone she can count on, not a stranger."

I was beginning to hate the word *family*! With Dad and his brothers and sisters, *family* was all-important. I was sick of too many family dinners and picnics and gossip and opinions and nobody minding their own business. The family had decided that my summer plans were the least important, so I was stuck with having to do a job none of them probably wanted.

"Why couldn't Uncle Gabe have been careful? Why'd he have to fall down the stairs and break his ankle?" I muttered to myself.

But Mom heard. "It's just lucky that's all that happened," she said. "Glenda was thankful that he hadn't been killed." She turned to my father. "Michael, why don't you go onto the Internet and buy Julie's ticket, and I'll help her get ready to pack."

It wasn't my choice. I didn't even have a vote in what was happening to my life. I had only one day to resign from the swim team, tell my best friend, Robin Norwich, that I'd keep in touch by e-mail, wash everything in my closet that Mom thought ought to be washed, and pack.

Aunt Glenda wasn't kidding when she said the road was winding. I clung to the armrest on the door and tried to brace myself against the swerves and bumps. I could tell we were climbing higher and higher. At one point the car dipped and we drove through shallow water. I could hear it splashing against the underside.

"That's our creek," Aunt Glenda said. "It's usually not even ankle deep, except after a big rain, when it's swollen. Then no one can drive in or out."

"Can't someone build a bridge?" I asked. My question made sense to me, but Aunt Glenda gave a strange laugh.

"What, and spoil all this rustic wonderfulness?" she said. She didn't smile. In fact, she looked positively grim, so I decided not to ask any more questions.

We rounded another curve, and to my right I saw a house. A porch light was on, and although the downstairs seemed dark, there were lights in two of the rooms upstairs. A wide porch stretched across the front of the house, and it looked welcoming.

"I like your house," I said.

Glenda gave a quick glance to the right, then said, "That's not our house. That's where Mabel and Harvey McBride live."

Startled, I said, "I thought this was *your* ranch."

"Oh, no," Glenda said. "We only own ten acres. We've got one of the smallest spreads. The McBrides own twenty-five acres, and I think Ann and Eugene Barrow own the largest spread—fifty acres. There are twenty retired couples who own spreads in Rancho del Oro."

"I don't understand," I told her. "How can each of you own separate ranches if this is all one big ranch?"

"You'll have to get your uncle Gabe to explain it all to you," she said. "It has to do with taxes. We invest in Rancho del Oro, which is a working ranch. We select property and can build on it, but otherwise we don't interfere with the cattle that live on the ranch, which means we can't build fences or grow tall hedges or even shoo them away. When cattle are sold, we either make a joint profit or we take a joint loss. If it's a loss, then at least there's a tax write-off."

"Is that why you moved here from Dallas?" I asked.

"For me, yes. The only reason." She looked even grimmer.

I thought about Glenda's success as an interior designer and how surprised Mom and Dad and all the aunts and uncles had been when she'd given it up. "Did you want to retire from the design center?" I asked.

Glenda made a strange noise that was almost a groan, almost a sob, but she tried to smile. "Your questions are getting a bit personal, sweetie."

"I'm sorry," I said. "I only—" I stopped speaking as Aunt Glenda slammed on the brakes. Directly in front of her car stood a very large cow.

The cow rolled her eyes in fright and let out a terrifying bellow. It was so loud I clapped my hands over my ears. Then I reached for the door handle. "I'll get out and see if it's hurt," I said.

"I didn't even touch it," Aunt Glenda told me. "I think it's just scared."

The cow kept her big eyes on us, this time with a look of reproach. She let out another bellow and moved off the road into the darkness.

"It made an awful sound," I said. "I thought cows just said 'Moo.'"

Aunt Glenda shook her head. "On their better days they make a noise that sounds like a baritone with a sinus infection."

We both laughed, and I began to like this great-aunt, who would never win prizes for her driving ability but seemed to have a good sense of humor.

As Aunt Glenda continued to drive toward home, she pointed out landmarks, such as the clubhouse with its swimming pool, and the stables. I stretched to get a glimpse of the pool area and began to feel a little better about the way I was going to spend my summer vacation. I wouldn't have to give up swimming. I could do my daily laps and stay in practice. Maybe I could still be on the team when I got home.

But the creepy feelings returned as we reached the end of the road and turned into a long driveway. The house was low and spread out, just one story. But at one end, over the carport, was a small towerlike room, with shrouded windows all around and a steep stairway on the outside wall.

Aunt Glenda saw me staring up at the tower as we climbed from the car, and she stopped, resting a hand on my shoulder. "That's a room your uncle Gabe added. He outfitted it as an observatory," she said. "He loves to study the stars. That's his hobby."

She sighed, and I could feel the tremor in her fingers as she lowered her voice. "He fell on those stairs. He said something was there to trip him. His shoe caught on something, and he tripped. But later, when we looked, we couldn't find anything that might have caused him to fall." She gripped my shoulder more tightly. "Of course he's wrong in thinking it wasn't an accident. But he has always been careful, Julie, so I can't help wondering . . ."

I tried to make sense of what she had said. If Uncle Gabe's fall hadn't been an accident, as he'd insisted, then something had caused him to fall. If it hadn't been found, then it must have been taken away. In this lonely, secluded place, why would something like that happen, and who could have done it?

As I took my suitcase and laptop from the car and followed Aunt Glenda to the front door of her house, I couldn't resist looking over my shoulder into the darkness. I realized I already missed the city sounds of Santa Monica, the echoes of traffic from the highway, the occasional sirens down on the boulevard, and the seagulls' cries. This lonely place in Texas was smothered in a deadly silence that scared me a little.

I made a dash through the open door of the house, slamming and locking it tightly behind us.

Chapter
Two

IN SPITE OF THE TWO-HOUR TIME DIFFERENCE BETWEEN
California and Texas, I awoke early Monday morning to
see gray streaks of light soaking up the night sky. As I
stood at my bedroom window, gazing across a wide
clearing into a vine-tangled mass of scrub and oak, a
deer came into view. Stepping delicately, like a prima
ballerina, the doe hesitated and glanced to each side.
Seemingly satisfied, she bent to nibble the cropped
plants at her feet.

I slid open the window to get a better view, but she
saw me and raised her head. For one quick instant she
stared into my eyes; then she turned and bounded out
of sight. A large black crow swooped down from the
trees, cawing and scolding, and the spell was broken.

I glanced at the clock: 5:45. Glenda had told me the
pool opened at six, so I fumbled in my suitcase for my
swimsuit. I'd unpack the rest of my clothes later. I was
eager to swim laps before breakfast.

Wearing tennies and pulling a T-shirt over my suit, I

quietly picked up the car keys Glenda had given me. I walked down the hall past the master bedroom and another guest bedroom and through the living room, with its muted blue-and-gray sofa and big easy chairs, and left the house. Still awed by the silence of this place, I drove down to the pool area and parked. I tried the door of the pool office to see if I had to sign in, but it was locked, and no one was inside. Two sides of the room were windows, so it was easy to see inside. The walls were stark white and bare, except for a calendar. A white metal desk that faced the door held a computer and a messy clutter of papers. At one side of the room, looking totally out of place, was a lumpy red plaid sofa.

I walked through the open gate to the pool, and to my disappointment, I wasn't alone. It was only two minutes after six, but a cluster of white swim caps already dotted the shallow end of the pool.

The chatter stopped when the swimmers spied me.

"Yoo-hoo," someone called. "Are you here to join our water exercise class?"

I quickly walked to their end of the pool and looked down on a dozen smiling faces, all of them sun-dotted with reflections from the water and haloed with white rubber. One swim cap even had ruffled flowers on it.

"I'm Julie Hollister," I told them. "I'm here visiting my father's aunt and uncle, Glenda and Gabe Hollister."

"Oh, your darling aunt!"

"She'll be so glad to have company."

"How awful for Gabe to take that terrible fall!"

"I said those stairs looked dangerous. Didn't I, Mabel? Don't you remember my saying it?"

The babble went on, growing in intensity, until a tall, lean, and bronzed King of the Swimming Pool, wearing the briefest of swim trunks, strode up and quietly ordered, "Settle down, ladies. We're ready to get started."

What a total hunk! I almost joined the exercise class myself. But I was here to swim laps, not work on tightening my stomach muscles with a bunch of grandmothers. I excused myself and dove into the deep end of the pool. After I got over the shock of the cold water, which was not yet warmed by the sun, I swam short laps and made plans. With the exercisers taking up the east end of the pool, I wouldn't be able to swim long laps, but at least I could keep up with some of my regular workout program. I'd find out what days the exercise ladies met and time my swimming so I'd have the pool to myself.

Half an hour later, as I toweled myself dry, I read the posted schedule near the office door. It listed the 6:00 A.M. exercise class only on Mondays, Wednesdays, and Fridays and gave the time the pool was open each day of the week. I quickly glanced at the few other notices that had been tacked on the board. A faded-ink file card, dated in early May, offered a $50 reward for Betty Jo Crouch's lost gold and diamond watch. The club was taking reservations for next Sunday's evening buffet. A restaurant, a cleaning service, and a dentist in Kerrville had tacked up business cards.

When I returned to the house, Glenda had set up the toaster, had placed a package of frozen waffles beside it, and had poured orange juice for the two of us. I showered and dressed quickly, knowing that as soon as we had finished eating, we'd go to the hospital to visit Uncle Gabe.

"Now, don't mind if he seems a bit out of sorts," Glenda warned me as we arrived at the hospital. "He's bound to want to tell you all about how his fall wasn't an accident. I'm sure he's wrong, but don't argue. Just listen and be patient."

I wasn't about to argue with anybody.

The Kerrville hospital was tiny compared to our supersized St. John's Hospital in Santa Monica, but it featured the same gleaming white walls and tile floors, and corridors onto which opened endless identical doors.

Gabe was propped in bed, supported by two over-sized pillows. Attached to him was an IV bag that hung on a hook near the right side of the bed.

His eyes lit up when he saw me. "Glad you could come, Julie," he said. "I didn't want your aunt Glenda on her own, after what happened."

"Nonsense," Glenda said. She took a step toward the bed and smoothed the wrinkled blanket. "If you'd put out of your mind what happened to you, your blood pressure might settle down and they'd let you go home."

"Fool doctors," Gabe muttered. He scratched the top of his bald head. "My blood pressure would go down by itself if they'd just let me out of here. I need to find out what made me take that nosedive on the stairs."

Glenda spoke softly, as though soothing a child. "It was an accident, dear. I searched the stairs. There was nothing on them to make you trip."

"Maybe you didn't want to find anything," Gabe grumbled.

As Glenda rolled her eyes, he raised himself on an elbow, grunting with the effort, and leaned toward me. "Julie's young," he said. "She's got sharp eyes. Julie can take a good look at those stairs, and I bet she'll find something. You'll search them carefully, won't you, Julie?"

"Now, Gabe," Glenda began, patience stretching her words into extra syllables.

"Sure, Uncle Gabe," I said. "The minute we get back, I'll examine the stairs."

He relaxed against the pillows, a satisfied smirk on his face. "That's all I want, Julie. Glenda keeps telling me I fell because I'm getting old. Well, maybe I can't stop time, but I do know that my age had nothing to do with my fall. Whatever tripped me did."

Glenda bent to kiss his forehead. "Is there anything you want or need before we leave?" she asked.

Gabe bellowed, "What? You're leaving already? You just got here."

Glenda patted his shoulder. "I'd stay here all day, Gabe, if you needed me. Honestly, I would. But I promised to attend the goodbye luncheon for Betty Jo Crouch, and Ann—who's giving the party—absolutely insisted I was to bring Julie. She wouldn't hear otherwise."

Gabe's lower lip stuck out, just like my little brother Trevor's when he's pouting, but Gabe said, "I just want to go home."

"Then stop fretting and carrying on about your fall," Glenda told him. "Julie will examine the stairs. She told you she would."

Gabe scowled at Glenda, then turned to look at me solemnly. "I'm counting on you," he said.

"I'll look the minute we get home," I told him.

I was true to my promise, although after all Glenda had told me, I really didn't expect to find anything. While Glenda was in the house making last-minute touch-ups to her hair and makeup, I took a close look at the stairs leading up to the room Uncle Gabe called his observatory. I decided to look at the area as if I were Sherlock Holmes.

The outer coat of paint, which matched the pale blue-green trim on the house, was fresh and thick. I looked hard and noticed two tiny nail holes in the supports at each side of the top step. Were they there by mistake? They were about four inches above the step and so small they'd be hard for anyone to notice. I wondered if anyone would even be able to find them after a few more weeks of weathering. I imagined a string—maybe clear plastic fishing line—stretched across from nail to nail.

Carefully, I searched the dusty cement slab below the stairway. I couldn't find anything. There was no trace of nails, or fishing line, or whatever might have been on the stairs.

Had something really been there that made Uncle Gabe trip and fall? I tried to discount the suspicion, but I actually could answer *yes*. Someone might have tried to trip Gabe at the head of the stairs. Who would do it? Why? These questions without answers made me uncomfortable.

I didn't tell Glenda what I might have found. First, I needed to think about what it meant.

* * *

Everyone at the luncheon was dressed in frilly, flowery cotton prints, so that Mrs. Barrow's large living room resembled a florist's shop. I had seen some of the women that morning at the pool, only now their hair was teased and curled and no longer hidden by swim caps.

Before we'd arrived at the goodbye luncheon, Glenda had told me about the Crouches and what had recently happened. While Betty Jo Crouch had been shopping in Kerrville, her husband, Albert, had apparently lost his balance and fallen to his death from their back porch into the ravine below. Mrs. Crouch and her visiting cousin had found him when they returned. "Just a little over three weeks ago on a Wednesday," Glenda had said. "Poor Betty Jo."

Betty Jo Crouch was dabbing at her eyes and complaining that she should have insisted Albert go shopping with them, as had been planned. She shouldn't have let him use the excuse of that teeny little argument to stay home. She managed to smile at Glenda and the other women, who—sherry glasses in hand—had circled her protectively.

"My daughter and four beautiful grandchildren and all my lifelong friends live in Beaumont," Mrs. Crouch bubbled. And she went on about how active she'd been in her garden club and her Gray Lady work in the Beaumont hospital's gift shop. "Of course, I'll get involved again, the very minute they sign me up," she said, unable to hide her eagerness to leave.

She reached for another glass of sherry from a tray being passed by a woman whose plump body was encased in a dark blue dress and a ruffled white apron. Her dyed orange hair was pulled taut to the nape of her neck and fastened with a rubber band.

"Thank you, Millie Lee," Mrs. Crouch said, and sighed.

"Brenda will be here soon to help me pack, thank goodness," Mrs. Crouch continued. "She'll help me find everything—"

"What do you mean, find everything?" Dorothy Templeton, the lady to her left, interrupted.

Mrs. Crouch blushed. "Oh, I suppose it's my age. At least that's what Albert kept telling me. Sometimes I forget where I put things for safekeeping." Her voice dropped. "Like the blue topaz ring Albert gave me for our last anniversary."

"And you misplaced your gold and diamond watch," Mrs. Templeton added. "You pinned up a notice on the board by the swimming pool."

"I can't imagine where I left that watch," Mrs. Crouch said. "I'd been at the pool and put my things on the table down at the far end." Again she sighed. "I just can't remember if I had my watch with me. That's the problem."

"It's not age," Mrs. Barrow said. "Everyone mislays something once in a while."

Donna Anderson said, "Maybe it's because we live out here on the ranch. Our lives are so totally different. We don't have dressy occasions to go to. I can't remember the last time I wore my favorite opal and diamond pendant."

She suddenly looked sheepish. "For that matter," she almost mumbled, "I don't even remember where I put it."

Mabel McBride, who had introduced herself to me

earlier, sighed loudly and added, "This ranch life may suit some of you, but as for me, I'd like to be back in my old neighborhood, near my children and grandchildren."

Ann Barrow picked up a heavy brass paperweight with an oil company logo on it. "It was so nice when Eugene was still a CEO and liked his job and kept busy at it," she said sadly. "We'd go to the Broadway road shows when they came to Houston. We never missed a symphony. And we had yearly subscriptions to the Alley Theatre."

She thumped down the paperweight and frowned. "I keep this on the table by the fireplace to remind myself of what life used to be like."

"Ralph always points out that our ranch investment was a marvelous financial opportunity." A tiny woman with a bad permanent spoke up timidly.

Mabel laughed and said, "Along with cow patties on our front walks and rattlers in our woodpiles and a tenmile drive to the nearest grocery store."

"Rancho del Oro has its good points, too," the timid woman said. "In the early morning, from the top of our hill, you can see the mist rising from row after row of purple hills, a benediction in the early sunlight."

"Oh, hush, Lila," somebody said.

Ann Barrow turned to me, a wry twist to her mouth. "Lila Grady is an artist," she said. "She doesn't see things the way we do. She keeps telling us that beauty is all around us."

Millie Lee was called to bring more sherry, but she cut off the request by announcing that lunch was served. The mood of the party didn't improve. I was hungry, so I wolfed down the chicken salad. My aunt hinted that I should help Millie Lee clear the plates and serve the chocolate mousse. So I did.

As I scraped the plates in Mrs. Barrow's kitchen, Millie Lee said, "This isn't the first time the ladies have let go about feelin' sorry for themselves. Believe me, they don't quit rememberin' what life was like before they moved here. Them bein' on this ranch is like a bunch of mice caught in a trap. Often, when I clean their houses, they confide in me. Ain't nothin' I haven't heard before."

She pulled a large pitcher of iced tea out of the refrigerator as she said, "I can sympathize. I know how they feel about livin' where they don't want to live because I got shunted around from place to place, through no wish of my own. My husband, Jimmy Don Kemp—may he rest in peace, though I doubt he will—was an oil-field driller, and we spent our whole married life on the move. It wasn't a picnic, always leavin' friends and havin' to make new ones, and he never understood why I'd sometimes cry into my pillow late at night. Everythin' had to be his way or nothin'."

Her voice sounded bitter. I was startled when it changed quickly and she suddenly went back to being good-tempered and friendly. "I've got a granddaughter 'bout your age who'll be with me for the summer." She turned to study me. "You fifteen? Sixteen?"

"Sixteen."

She smiled, satisfied. "So's Ashley. Maybe you and she could get together sometimes."

"Sure," I answered. I looked forward to having someone my own age to talk to.

"Miz Hollister worried that by coming here you'd miss your friends back home."

"It's okay," I said. "We can keep in touch by e-mail. My best friend and I are on each other's buddy lists, so we can instant-message each other as often as we're both online."

"I know kids love the Internet," Millie Lee said as she nodded. "But sometimes it's better to have people on hand you can look at and talk to. While you're here, you and Ashley can get together. I'll bring her to work with me tomorrow."

After the luncheon, when we returned to Glenda's house, I told her about Millie Lee's granddaughter. "Would you mind if I invited her over?" I asked.

"I'd love to have the two of you make friends," Glenda said. "I've met Ashley Kemp, and she's a dear girl." Glenda gave me a quick glance, then said, "Just between you and me, Ashley doesn't know who her father is, more's the pity. And every now and then her mother takes off for a couple of months, so Ashley moves in with her grandmother. She comes to work with Millie Lee, and I try to make her feel welcome because I'm not sure Millie Lee knows how to."

"What is Ashley like?" I asked.

"I just told you. I—"

"No, Aunt Glenda. I mean is she tall or short? Does she like to swim? Does she read a lot? Does she jog?"

"Oh, goodness," Glenda said. "I know she's probably an inch or two shorter than you, but then you come from the tall side of the family. And she has red hair—real red, not out of the bottle like her grandmother. And freckles. She's pretty, but she's a little too thin, if you ask me, although I know you girls always think you can't be thin enough. As for what she likes to do, you'll have to find out for yourself."

"Tomorrow," I said.

"That's right. Tomorrow morning."

Glenda unfastened the beautiful string of baroque pearls she was wearing and pulled off her pearl ear clips. "I'm going to take a little nap," she said. "You can find something to occupy you for an hour or so, can't you?"

I nodded. "I've brought my laptop. If it's all right with you, I'll connect it."

"Of course," Glenda said. "If you'd rather, you can use mine. I keep it on a side table in Gabe's office." She looked apologetic as she added, "It's a few years old and I've never updated the modem so it's not very fast."

"Thanks," I said, "but I'm used to mine."

She smiled. "I know you'll want to e-mail your parents and let them know you arrived here safely."

"Oh, yes. I guess," I said. I couldn't help feeling a little guilty. "I was thinking about my best friend," I said. "We instant-message each other." Before Glenda could say anything I added, "I'll write to Mom, too."

Glenda just smiled and said, "You can set your laptop up on Gabe's desk in his study. He won't be using the study for a good long while, so you can just keep it there, if you like." She paused at the doorway. "Later this afternoon we'll go back to the hospital to visit Gabe and then stop for something to eat at a restaurant near the hospital. You do like Italian food, don't you?"

I told her I did. As she shut the door to her bedroom, I quietly left the living room through the front door and walked around the side of the house to re-examine the steps to Uncle Gabe's observatory room. Even with all the distractions the day had brought, I'd kept thinking about those nail holes. Were they real? Or had I imagined them? If they were real, I'd have to tell Uncle Gabe about them.

They were real, all right. I sat on the top step, trying to think things through. What should I do?

I didn't want to tell Glenda. It would only frighten her, and I had no proof of what I suspected—that something had been tied between those nails to trip Gabe. I certainly didn't want to tell Mom or Dad about it. It would be like yelling for help, expecting them to drop whatever they were doing and come running, and they had already made it clear that their work was too important to be interrupted—much more important than anything *I* had planned.

There *was* someone I could talk this over with—my best friend, Robin. She'd be perfect. Sometimes I teased her for being such an ardent fan of mystery novels. Maybe Robin would know if what I had found meant anything. Maybe she'd know what I should do next.

When I returned to the house, I stopped off at the kitchen and took a soft drink out of the refrigerator. I glanced around the room, which was pale yellow and white, cheerful and efficient, with new-looking appliances. It had very little clutter, except for a scattering of ceramic hens and roosters on the windowsill and what looked like a kid's bank. It was a small ceramic two-story building with DIME BOX painted across the roof. In the center of the kitchen table stood a brightly woven basket filled with fruit. I touched a shiny apple, and it was real. Good. If Glenda didn't mind, I'd enjoy eating some of her centerpiece.

I carried my laptop into Gabe's wood-paneled study. The walls lent their deep brown tones to the brown patterned drapes and thick brown carpeting. The desk and chairs were also brown, and I began to get the crazy feeling that I was being sucked into a dark old tree trunk. Quickly, I plugged in my laptop and the screen lit up. I went into my ISP.

"You've got mail," a friendly voice announced, but before clicking on the mailbox icon, I saw Robin's name on my buddy list. She was already online, so I ignored my mail and sent her an instant message.

Jul59: Hi, Robin. Got a minute?
Robinor: Hi yourself. Just a few minutes. Swim-team practice, you know. Tell me, what's the ranch like? Meet any good-looking cowboys?
Jul59: No cowboys, but there's a kind of mystery. You're the mystery expert. Want to help?
Robinor: K. Tell me about it.
Jul59: K. Here goes. I'll just give important points. Uncle Gabe fell down a flight of outside stairs. He said something tripped him. Aunt Glenda said it didn't. He asked me to look. I did and found two nail holes near the top step. I believe a string could have been tied between them and taken away later. I suspect that it was. Am I crazy? What do I do?
Robinor: You haven't even been there 24 hours and wow! Action! K. Who has access to the stairs?

Jul59: I don't know. Anybody. They're outside.

Robinor: Did you find the string?

Jul59: No. And I looked all around and under the stairs. Nothing.

Robinor: You are not crazy as far as I know! Look for WHO and WHY. There has to be a reason. You know, a motive. Every crime has a motive. Do you suspect anyone?

Jul59: No. I don't even know many people here yet.

Robinor: Talk to your great-uncle. Try to find out if anyone has something against him.

Jul59: It might be hard to come right out and ask him. He has high blood pressure, and Glenda doesn't want him to get excited.

Robinor: When he gets home from the hospital, can he get up the stairs to see the nail holes for himself?

Jul59: No. He has a broken ankle.

Robinor: You make it tough, girl. I gotta go now. POS. Give me time to think about this. In the meantime, if you can't question your uncle, then look for other people who might answer your questions. K?

Jul59: K. Thanks, Robin.

In a way, there was a parent over my shoulder, too—Mom. I knew there'd be a letter from her, so I clicked on the e-mail icon. Just as I did, a hand touched my shoulder. I let out a yell and leaped out of my chair.

Glenda stared at me in surprise. "I'm sorry I startled you," she said. "I thought you heard me come into the room."

"I didn't," I answered. My face turned red as I wondered if she'd been reading over my shoulder. "When did you come in?"

"Just this minute," she said. "I couldn't sleep. Too much sherry does that to me." She held out her car keys in my direction. "If you don't mind, I think we should go visit Gabe now. That way we'll be home before dark."

As I took the keys, my fingers trembled. I didn't know Aunt Glenda well enough to be sure she was telling me the truth.

But if she had read what Robin and I had written to each other, she'd know that we suspected someone of causing Gabe's accident, and she'd ask me about it.

Wouldn't she?

I hated the fact that I had no way of knowing.

Chapter
Three

THE FIRST THING UNCLE GABE SAID TO ME AS WE WALKED INTO his hospital room was "Did you get a chance—?"

"Of course she didn't," Glenda interrupted. "I told you, we went to a luncheon, and then we took naps."

"Teenage girls don't take naps," Gabe grumbled.

"I set up my laptop," I told him. I didn't want to bring up my discovery of the nail holes. I wasn't sure why they were there. I didn't want anyone to know about anything suspicious until I had more information. Like maybe knowing *who* and *why.* Robin said I had to find out. She was the one who knew how mysteries were solved. I had to start somewhere.

"Uncle Gabe," I said, "tell me how Rancho del Oro is operated. I mean, are there cowboys and a chuck wagon and all the things we see in Westerns?"

Gabe smiled and patted the side of his bed, motioning for me to sit down. Glenda had taken the only chair in the room, so I perched on the edge of the bed and listened.

"There's a ranch manager, name of Martin Cooper," Gabe said. "He keeps the books and arranges the purchases and sales of the cattle and the sales of the residences. He takes care of all the financial details and keeps us updated by e-mail."

"Does he live on the ranch, too?"

"No. He lives in Dallas, where the corporation is headquartered. As a matter of fact, he doesn't put in an appearance at the ranch very often, but when he comes, he usually flies in his private jet."

I was puzzled. "To the San Antonio airport?"

Grinning proudly, Gabe said, "We've got our own strip for small jets built on the highest point on the ranch. I take it that Glenda didn't do any sightseeing with you."

"I can't do everything at once," Glenda said in an aggrieved tone. "I plan to show Julie around the entire area soon as I get a chance."

Trying to distract them from another argument, I quickly asked, "If the ranch manager isn't at the ranch, then who takes care of the cattle?"

"The ranch foreman, Cal Grant," Gabe answered. "And he has three cowhands to help him. Nice people. All of them up from Mexico with green cards. Perfectly legal. One of them has a son in high school named Luis who was born here. In the summer and on weekends during the year, Luis hires himself out for small repairs around the houses, or weeds the flower beds, or paints trim—things like that."

He gripped the sheet and blanket in frustration as he turned to Glenda. "That reminds me. Get Luis in to clean out that trap under the kitchen sink. That was next on my list of things to do, and now there's no way I can take care of it."

Glenda nodded. "I'll call Luis. Don't you worry about it."

"Do it right away. You're going to be cooking more than usual when I get home and—"

"But not tonight," she said. "Julie and I plan to take it easy and eat out. Italian."

Uncle Gabe looked like a little kid who'd been told he hadn't been invited to a birthday party. "Fried ravioli," he said quietly. "Shrimp scampi. Tiramisu."

"None of which is good for you," Glenda said briskly. She kissed the top of his head. "As soon as your blood pressure comes down, the doctor said we can take you home."

About fifteen minutes later, in a cozy little Italian restaurant, Glenda added, "Tonight I'm going to indulge in something with lots of cheese and calories. After we bring Gabe home, I'll go back to healthful meals that suit his diet." She looked at the menu and sighed with pleasure.

I'd found out enough information to know how the ranch operated, but I couldn't ask Gabe anything that might cause his blood pressure to go up. I decided to try to get more information from Glenda. After we had ordered, I leaned my elbows on the table and asked her, "Is there anyone at the ranch who might be . . . well, angry at Uncle Gabe?"

She looked puzzled. "Angry? Well, Gabe tends to be a little blunt and is usually likely to grumble about something or other—" she began.

She suddenly stopped, narrowed her eyes, and gave me a piercing look. "Wait a minute," she said. "Are you going along with Gabe's crazy idea that somebody did something to cause him to fall down the stairs?"

I must have looked guilty, because she said, "Humor Gabe, but please don't get caught up in his fantasy, Julie."

I decided it would be best to change the subject. "Tell me about the job you used to have at the design center," I said.

The expression on Glenda's face went from delight, as she described some of the homes she had decorated, to wistfulness, as she spoke about the impossibility of continuing her work after they had moved to the ranch.

Our salads arrived, and she seemingly forgot the question she had asked me.

I was glad. I didn't want to give her an answer.

But I thought about it later that evening, after Glenda had gone to bed and I'd returned to my laptop to finally read my e-mail.

The first was from Mom, dated the day before and written the moment I'd left:

Darling Julie,

Your dad and I can't thank you enough for giving up your summer to help the family. E-mail us often, love. Keep us informed. We miss you. When Uncle Gabe gets home from the hospital, be sure he remembers to take his medicine. Write down the dosage and the times he takes it and fasten it to the refrigerator, where the list is easily seen. That's the best way.

Hugs and kisses, Mom

Make a list. Fine. I had just gotten here and I was getting instructions from the family already.

So far there wasn't anything to write about, so I just answered:

Everything OK. Love, Julie

Following was an e-mail from my aunt Ellen:

Hi, Julie.

You're a good kid to step in and help. Thanks. Be sure Gabe takes his pills at the time he's supposed to do so. I found, when my children were young, that keeping a detailed chart is best.

She went on to describe how to make a grid for days of the week and times of the day, as if I were five years old. I groaned and clicked on **Reply**, then wrote:

Will do. Julie and clicked on **Send Now**.

The next letter was from Aunt Samantha, who wrote:

Dear Julie,

We're leaving for London tomorrow, and then on to Paris next week. It should be a glorious trip, but I can't help worrying about Gabe and Glenda. We're all so glad they're in your capable hands. Please be sure that Gabe takes his medications when he's supposed to. A timer is the best way to do it. If Glenda doesn't have a kitchen timer, you can buy one at the nearest drugstore. If there's a discount store, try that first. I'm telling you all this because Glenda may not own a timer. I've heard her complain that she's spent a lifetime cooking and she's tired of it. Also, make sure they both get their naps after lunch.

Scowling at the computer, I sent Aunt Samantha the same message I'd sent Aunt Ellen. Why did everyone in the family think they had to tell me what to do?

The next two messages were from stores I'd never shopped in, but somehow they'd gotten hold of my e-mail address. I deleted their ads without opening them.

The last was an e-mail from Robin asking me what I'd found out.

I e-mailed back: **Nothing.**

I was about to shut down when I heard a familiar jingle and the buddy screen popped up.

Robinor: Nothing at all? What did you talk about?
Jul59: About who manages the ranch and who runs it.
Robinor: You should be here, not there. Our swim-team practice was horrible. We don't stand a chance without you.
Jul59: It's not my fault I'm not on the swim team this summer. You know that.
Robinor: I know. Sorry. I didn't mean to upset you. BFF?
Jul59: BFF. There's a pool here. I'll try to practice. Talk to you tomorrow.

BFF. Best friends forever. I closed my laptop feeling a wave of disappointment. I had hoped Robin would give me the help I needed to decide what to do about Uncle Gabe. How could she, really? She was far away. I walked through Gabe's study, turning off the light as I left.

As I flipped off the table lamp in the living room, I sensed movement behind the wide windows and froze. Again I saw a shift in the night's pattern of faint light and deep black. Someone was outside, near the window.

I inched toward the windows, keeping my back to the wall. When I was close enough, I pressed my face to the glass and squinted into the night.

Something raised a massive head and looked back at me, almost nose to nose. Too startled to even make a sound, I staggered backward, falling over the back of the sofa into its cushions, where I lay without moving, my heartbeat slowly returning to normal.

A cow. The thing outside the window was nothing more than a big-eyed, wide-mouthed, shaggy-faced cow. I remembered what we'd learned in history a few years ago about cows being sacred in India. Well, they seemed to be just as sacred here on Rancho del Oro.

I climbed off the sofa and tried another window. There were three cows out there, each of them munching away at Glenda's bushes and flowers, and I couldn't even shoo them off. Tomorrow that part of the garden would be gone, and in its place would be a scattering of cow patties. It was easy to understand why the ladies I'd heard complain at lunch hated the cows, who had first rights.

I could see through the dark well enough to make my way back to the guest bedroom. It didn't take long to get ready for bed. I kept thinking about what I should do next to find out what or who had caused Gabe's fall.

Tomorrow, I told myself. I'll think about it tomorrow. Tonight I was exhausted. I closed my eyes and fell asleep.

Early the next morning I had the pool to myself. Not even the Hunk was there.

Once again, the cold water was a shock, and because the altitude was a little over fifteen hundred feet higher than Santa Monica's sea level, I breathed heavily, gasping gulps of air instead of sucking them in smoothly. But as I swam laps back and forth, I felt at home in the water. The kinks began to leave both my body and my mind, and an idea surfaced—an idea worth investigating.

I showered and joined Glenda for breakfast, which consisted of a carton of orange juice and a formerly frozen egg-and-cheese dish in a small plastic casserole. Cooked to bubbling in the microwave, the mixture didn't taste exactly like eggs or like cheese, but it was edible, and I scarfed down my half, mopping up the last crumb with a slice of toast. The strange little DIME BOX bank caught my eye. I wanted to ask Glenda about it, but she was intent on telling me all about the women I'd met the day before.

"I think Mabel's older than she'll admit," Glenda said. "She's always losing things or misplacing them. Goodness knows what she does with them or where she puts them. Two weeks ago it was her gold bracelet. Yesterday she said she couldn't find her emerald ring. I just hope I never get so scatterbrained . . ."

I wasn't really interested in Mabel McBride's state of mind, so at that point I tuned Glenda out and concentrated on my breakfast.

As I took our plates to the sink, the back door swung open and Millie Lee stepped into the kitchen. "Mornin', y'all," she said.

"Morning, Millie Lee," Glenda answered. She beamed. "And good morning to you, Ashley."

Just behind Millie Lee appeared a girl with freckles across her nose and a mop of curly red hair. Ashley Kemp. Just as Glenda had described her. "Hi," I said.

Millie Lee smiled proudly, but Ashley's face was solemn, even a little wary, as she looked at me.

"This is my granddaughter I told you about," Millie Lee said.

"Hi," I said again. "I'm Julie."

Ashley still didn't smile. For an instant the four of us were trapped in one of those silences during which no one has a thing to say. Then we all started talking at once.

Millie Lee said, "Mostly Ashley helps me, but today she can do whatever you girls want to do."

"Maybe you'd like to play Chinese checkers. We have a game board in the den," Glenda said.

At the same time I blurted out, "Want to go swimming this afternoon, Ashley?"

Ashley was mumbling, "You probably have other things to do. Go ahead. I'll help Gran."

We were silent again as we all tried to sort out what we'd heard. I was the first to recover and came out with what had been on my mind since my early swim. "Aunt Glenda, I'd like to do some exploring. I haven't seen Uncle Gabe's observatory. Could Ashley and I take a look at his telescope?"

Glenda seemed relieved. "Of course," she answered. "Would you like that, Ashley?"

Ashley shrugged and nodded at the same time, which made her look like a turtle trying to escape into its shell.

Millie Lee looked a little nervous as Glenda removed the key to the observatory from the board near the back door. "I don't know if that's a good idea," she said. "There's a lot of expensive, breakable stuff up there, like that telescope. When the sun hits that brass, you can see the gleam a mile away. I once got fingerprints on it when I dusted, and Mr. Hollister like to have taken my head off."

"Oh, dear. He does get touchy," Glenda said. "But the girls won't hurt anything." She handed me the key. "They'll enjoy using the telescope. You don't have to use it just to look at stars. During the daytime you can use it to scan quite a bit of the countryside."

"If you say so, Miz Hollister," Millie Lee said. "But, Ashley, don't you go touchin' things you shouldn't touch. Especially that model of the planets, with all those little balls sticking out on wires."

"I'll be careful, Gran," Ashley said.

As soon as we were outside and out of hearing range, I laughed. "I wonder how old we have to get before people stop expecting us to break things," I said.

I assumed that Ashley would think it was funny, too, so I added, "Sometimes my parents drive me crazy. And it's not just parents. I've got aunts and uncles breathing down my neck about everything. I can't make a single decision without having to listen to everyone's opinion."

Ashley didn't smile. She turned and gave me the kind of look a person would give a plate of brussels sprouts when she was expecting a hamburger. Okay, I told myself. She doesn't want to be friendly. But maybe she'll come around. She's the only one my age on this ranch, so unless I want to spend all my time playing Chinese checkers with grandmothers . . .

I didn't have to finish the thought. We had reached the stairs. "Let's go up," I said. I gave Ashley my friendliest smile and ran up the stairs, unlocking the door when I reached the top.

She was right behind me, but we both stopped short when we entered the room. We stood still and stared.

The walls were windows, tall and wide, and the room glowed from the sunlight that filtered through their gauzy blinds. The model of planets that Millie Lee had spoken about rested on a small table in the center of the room. It seemed to focus the light, drawing it into each of its shining brass orbs.

"Wow!" Ashley said.

"Let's open the blinds," I suggested, and as we did, there was plenty of time to note the astronomy books on a low bookshelf, the gigantic poster of the Milky Way that covered the inside of the door, and the charts and diagrams that were spread across Uncle Gabe's desk.

When all the windows were uncovered, the room lost its mystic look. On the other hand, it gave us a gorgeous view.

"Look—down there," I said, and pointed. "There's the swimming pool and the clubhouse."

I moved to the telescope that rested on a large tripod near one of the windows and focused on the pool. A black sedan slid in and parked in front of the office, and the Hunk climbed out. He pulled off his sweats, tossed them into his car, then scratched his chest and yawned widely. I giggled. He had no idea he was being watched.

Swinging the telescope in the other direction, I could see the Crouches' home—at least the part facing the road. And not too far off someone on his knees, bent over as he pulled weeds in a small flower bed next to the Barrows' house. In the distance, looking like my brother Trevor's small Western action figures, rode two men on horseback. Ahead of them plodded a half dozen or so head of cattle.

"Do you want to take a turn?" I asked Ashley, and she silently moved to the telescope.

I noticed that she lingered on the pool area a little longer than on anyplace else and I grinned, thinking that the Hunk didn't know how much he was being appreciated.

"Bring your swimsuit tomorrow," I said. "We'll go swimming at the clubhouse pool."

Ashley turned and studied me. "You really want me to go swimming with you? You weren't just saying that to please my grandmother?"

Startled, I said, "I invited you to swim with me because I thought we'd have fun. You don't have to if you don't want to."

"I *do* want to." Ashley's cheeks reddened, and she looked down at her toes.

I backed up a few steps, sank into Gabe's heavily padded leather office chair, and leaned back, twirling from side to side. "We should come here at night," I said, "and look at the stars, like Uncle Gabe does."

"Great. I'd like that," Ashley said, suddenly animated. "I found some terrific astronomy sites on the Internet, using Gran's computer. It's hard to find time, though, when she's not on it."

I was surprised, and asked without thinking, "What does she use her computer for? Freecell? Solitaire?"

Ashley shook her head. "No, she likes chat rooms and instant messaging. She talks to people all over the country."

"How about you? Do you have computer friends too?" I asked.

"I don't like chat rooms," Ashley said. "I don't know the people in them and I don't want to write messages to someone I don't know."

"Me either," I said. "I do a lot of instant messaging, but it's to my best friend at home."

"I love to find out new things on the Internet, like at the astronomy sites," Ashley added, "but it will be even more exciting to see the night sky through a telescope. I didn't realize it was your uncle who had the telescope."

I was glad I'd brought up the idea, because for some reason it seemed important to me that I look through that telescope in the darkness. I'd taken a careful look around the office so that when I came after dark I'd know my way around. Maybe I'd discover that Gabe had seen something he wasn't supposed to see, and that was why someone . . .

But I thought about the deep, silent darkness that enveloped the ranch at night, and about the heavy-footed cattle with their curious eyes and huge faces, and I knew I'd be too scared to come to the observatory by myself.

If Gabe had been right, and someone had wanted him to trip at the head of the stairs, and I found out who did it—

"Are you cold?" Ashley asked me. She sounded puzzled. "You just shivered."

Chapter Four

AFTER LUNCH GLENDA RECEIVED A CALL FROM GABE'S doctor. The new medication was working, Gabe's blood pressure was down, and he could check out of the hospital at any time. Since plans had changed, Millie Lee moved on to her afternoon people, as she called them, taking Ashley with her. Glenda gave Ashley a big hug and made her promise to come to our house the next morning with a swimsuit.

As Millie Lee reminded Glenda that she was almost out of tile cleaner, Ashley said to me in a low voice, "I don't live here. They won't want me in their pool."

"No one will tell you to leave," I said. "You'll be my guest. You're welcome, Ashley. I want you to come."

She gave me a long look, but I noticed that she held her chin higher, and she tried to smile. "You don't know much about me," she said.

"I don't need to," I answered. "I'm glad to know someone here my age. We're going to enjoy the pool together." I grinned. "And you're going to meet the Hunk."

"I've met him already," she said. "He rents the trailer next to Gran's. He's our neighbor." She paused, then said, "I was there when he moved his stuff in. Some heavy gym equipment and a full-length mirror."

We both broke out laughing at the same time. "See you tomorrow," I said.

"What was so funny?" Glenda asked as she shut the door behind Millie Lee and Ashley.

"Girl stuff," I answered, and giggled again.

Glenda didn't ask for details, the way Mom would have. She smiled as she picked up her purse and handed me the car keys. She settled herself into the seat, and as I backed the car out of the drive and headed down the road, she said, "In order for Gabe to recuperate quickly, we'll have to do our best to keep him from becoming upset about anything. He needs calm and quiet."

I gave her a quick look, then turned back to the road. "That means I'm not to say anything about his fall on the stairs?"

Glenda sighed. "We can count on Gabe continuing to carry on about his fall not being an accident. He's bound to pester you, Julie. Ignore him. Please."

I wasn't sure how to reply, so I said, "Maybe his fall *wasn't* an accident."

Glenda suddenly gripped my arm. I was so startled I swung over the dividing line on the highway and back. Luckily, no traffic was coming toward us.

She said quickly, "I needed a relative . . . a friend . . . someone I could trust to just be around, to give me a little peace of mind. If there is something going on around here that shouldn't be, please don't stir it up, Julie. Please."

"You're afraid," I blurted out. "You really don't think Uncle Gabe's fall was an accident, do you?"

She waited a long time before answering. Then she said, "It really doesn't matter what I think. The doctor said Gabe's broken ankle will heal properly. He doesn't expect problems. Gabe's coming home, so everything will be all right."

Unless whoever caused him to fall decides to try again, I thought. I gave her a quick look and knew by the tightness and strain I saw in her face that for now I'd better keep that opinion to myself.

Later, on the way back from the hospital to Rancho del Oro, Gabe gave us a long, grouchy list of things he didn't like about the hospital. On occasion, he interrupted himself by reminding me about the speed limit (which I was observing), pointing out a truck that was a good quarter mile away, and worrying in general about the safety of the nation when kids could get driver's licenses at such an early age.

It took both of us to get him into the house and safely tucked into one of the comfortable living room chairs, with his feet propped up on a hassock and his crutches at hand.

Glenda turned to me. "Julie, please entertain your uncle Gabe while I get supper put together."

"I'll help you," I offered.

"What are we having?" Gabe asked.

"Beef stew," Glenda said.

"You'll need help," I insisted. "I can peel and slice the carrots, potatoes, and onions."

She shook her head. "No need," she said. "It all comes in a package. I just have to take it out of the freezer, put it in a skillet with a half cup of water, and let it simmer for ten minutes."

She disappeared into the kitchen, so I sat in a chair next to Gabe. "Ashley and I visited your observatory today," I told him. "It's beautiful."

He beamed. "Made it myself," he said, then added almost grudgingly, "Well, with a little help from Luis."

I smiled. "When do you usually visit your observatory?"

"At night, of course, after it's dark enough to clearly see the stars."

"Are you ever there in the daytime?"

"Sure. Once in a while," he said. "It's easier to go over my charts in the daylight than it is at night with the glare of electric lights. Old eyes, you know."

"When you're in your observatory in the daytime, do you ever use your telescope?"

Gabe nodded. "Once in a rare while. If the day's clear, I like to guess how far I can see."

"How about close at hand? Have you ever seen something unusual around the ranch property?"

"Unusual? Like what?" He sat up a little, shifting in his chair.

"I don't know," I answered.

"Well, I sure as shootin' don't know either, so what are you getting at?"

I wasn't certain how to answer. "I used your telescope this morning," I said. "I couldn't believe all the small details I could see. I watched someone working in a flower bed and someone over at the swimming pool."

"Yeah," he said, and smiled. "That's a great telescope. I decided if I was going to buy one, I might as well get only the best. Wait until you try it at night."

Suddenly he twisted to look toward the kitchen. Then he leaned forward and lowered his voice. "Now's a good time to tell me," he said. "Did you examine the stairs to the observatory? Did you find anything?"

Sooner or later I'd have to answer. I gulped down the lump of guilt that threatened to stick in my throat, deciding, in spite of how Glenda had cautioned me, to tell him now and get it over with. "Uncle Gabe," I said, "you asked me to search for something that might have caused your fall. I did. I found two tiny nail holes opposite each other on the supports at the top of the stairs, about four inches above the stair."

He frowned, looking puzzled. Then the idea hit him and he said, "Nails? With a string tied between them?"

"It could be," I answered. But I quickly added, "There was no sign of the nails themselves or of a string under the stairs. I looked carefully."

In spite of the cast on his foot and ankle, Uncle Gabe nearly bounced out of his chair, grabbing for his crutches. He winced and fell back into the chair, then grinned in triumph and bellowed at the top of his lungs, "Glenda! Where are you?"

Glenda came running into the living room, a wooden spoon still in her hand. "What's the matter?" she cried.

Uncle Gabe leaned back and folded his arms across his chest. With a smug look on his face, he announced,

"Glenda, call Deputy Sheriff Dale Foster. Tell him to get here before it turns dark. Tell him I've got proof that my fall wasn't an accident. Just as I've been saying, it looks like someone really did try to get rid of me!"

Chapter
Five

GLENDA'S FACE TURNED A GREENISH WHITE, AND SHE dropped into the nearest chair as if her legs had turned into Jell-O. She took a couple of deep breaths before she spoke. Scared by what I had unwittingly done to her, I was grateful that color was coming back into her cheeks and her voice was as strong as ever.

"Before I go making any fool calls that might embarrass us both, you'd better tell me what you're talking about," she said.

Gabe was so proud of himself for being right, he looked like a rooster puffing up to crow. "Julie found two small nail holes across from each other at the top of the stairs. If someone had hammered in a couple of nails and tied a string across them, I would never have noticed them there. I would have tripped and taken a header down the stairs. Which I did."

Glenda gave me a hurt, puzzled look as she asked, "Why didn't you tell *me* about this, Julie?"

I squirmed. I should have seen this coming. "I—I

wasn't sure what had happened. I thought I'd better ask Uncle Gabe. I didn't want to give you anything more to worry about. You were worried enough already." I managed to stop babbling and said, "I'm sorry, Aunt Glenda. I should have told you right away."

She stood, put down her spoon, and beckoned to me. "Show me," she said.

"What about calling our deputy sheriff?" Gabe said.

"That's up to you." Glenda shoved the cordless phone into his hands and marched out of the room.

I trotted after her, trying to catch up with her long stride. When we reached the stairs, we climbed them together, and I pointed out the tiny nail holes at the top. She measured their exact distance from the top step between thumb and pointer finger, then looked warily at me. "They match," she said.

For just an instant, her shoulders sagged and she seemed a dozen years older. But the moment passed quickly. Her back stiffened as she said, "Two nail holes don't really prove a thing."

"Then why are you afraid?" I asked.

"I honestly don't know," she told me. "Gabe was so insistent that something had tripped him, I think I let it influence me. I wasn't thinking rationally when I called the family for help. Later, as I began to calm down, I was sure that no one had tripped him, that he needed an excuse for growing old."

She glanced to each side and shuddered. "We're so alone out here," she said quietly. "It's silent and lonely during the day, but at night there are dozens of strange noises—a crack of a twig or a footfall—with no one there to have made them. Unless we have a full moon, it's as dark outside as a bottle of ink."

A marked car pulled up and stopped behind the Hollisters' cars in the carport. A sun-reddened man, dressed in khakis with an official patch on one broad shoulder, stepped from the car. He touched the brim of his western hat and said, "Mornin', Miz Hollister."

"You got here awfully quick, Dale," she said.

"Yep. I was right down the road when I got Gabe's call. He said there were some nail holes you wanted me to see?"

"Yes, please. Up here," Glenda said. "Dale Foster, this is Julie Hollister, our nephew's daughter."

He touched his hat brim again and said, "Pleased to meet you, ma'am."

"I'm glad to meet you, too," I said. I stood up quickly and hurried down the stairs as the deputy climbed them. There wouldn't be room for three of us there at the same time.

I watched Glenda point out the holes. Foster bent double to examine them, then rose, chuckling. "I wouldn't worry my head over those nail holes," he said. "There's a good reason why you didn't find the nails that made 'em or a string tied to 'em. It's 'cause there weren't any. Take a close look at the stairs. You'll find other empty nail holes." He pointed as he said, "Here . . . and over here. That happens when the builder's an amateur."

He stepped off the bottom step at this point, Glenda following.

Puzzled, I asked, "How can you tell that the builder was an amateur?"

The deputy let out a guffaw before he answered, "Your uncle Gabe was the builder. That's how I know."

"Oh." I could feel myself blushing.

"Drat!" Glenda cried. "I forgot the stew!" She took a couple of quick steps toward the house before she politely turned and said, "Dale, it's a pretty simple supper, but would you care to join us? We'd be happy to have you."

"No thanks," Foster said. "I've got to be gettin' back to the office."

As Glenda disappeared through the front door, Foster said to me, "All the men who live on Rancho del Oro retired from busy desk jobs. To keep from bein' bored to death, they try their hands at buildin' and paintin' and fixin' their own plumbin'." His face crinkled into a broad smile. "And they're not very good at it."

"But Uncle Gabe said something tripped him and made him fall."

Foster walked to his car and opened the door. I trailed after him. "Did you notice how steep those stairs are? Don't you think your aunt gave your uncle a hard time about climbin' up and down them at his age? He's got to have a good excuse for fallin'."

"Do you really think that's all it is—an excuse?"

"I showed you some of the other nail holes, didn't I?" he answered.

As he drove off, I walked back to the stairs and slowly climbed them again, this time looking for nail holes. I found even more than the deputy had pointed out. I couldn't miss them. The nails that had made them were good-sized, leaving holes that couldn't be completely filled by a primer coat, then paint. But the holes I had discovered at the top of the stairs had been made with tiny nails. They were not the same kind of holes at all. And they'd been made later, after the stairs had been painted.

Foster had come with the opinion that Gabe was just looking for an excuse. He either hadn't noticed what I had said about the nail holes, or he hadn't cared. But I cared.

There was one more question I had to ask Uncle Gabe.

The potatoes in the stew were mushy, the julienne strips of carrots and inchlong cuts of string beans were soggy, and the few pieces of beef were overcooked. But Glenda had baked a roll of baking-powder biscuits from a container and put together a salad of field greens to go with the package of frozen instant stew, so the meal wasn't too bad.

Glenda ate serenely, but Gabe wasn't in a very good mood. He didn't like what the deputy had reported.

As we ate, I said to Gabe, "I'm impressed that you built that room and staircase by yourself."

He looked up at me sharply. "*Practically* by myself," he said. "I told you I got Luis to help me."

"Luis Garcia," Glenda reminded me. "Miguel Garcia's son. Luis is in high school."

"Did you call Luis about fixing the sink?" Gabe asked.

Glenda nodded. "He's coming tomorrow morning," she said.

I turned to Gabe. I tried to make sense, although I wasn't sure what I was talking about. "Isn't it complicated building a room and stairs on a house? Don't you have to buy certain nails for one thing and other nails for other things?"

"No," he said. "You get nice long, sturdy nails, and that's all you need." He glanced in Glenda's direction and said, "The deputy may have been flummoxed about those nail holes, but he's wrong, and someday—when I can get around like before—I'll prove it."

Glenda rolled her eyes. "Deputy Sheriff Foster gave us his opinion, so no more talk about nail holes," she said. "It's over and done with."

I bent over my plate so she wouldn't see the doubt in my eyes. It wasn't over and done with. I now believed those tiny nail holes hadn't been made by Gabe or Luis. Someone else had put them there. They were a totally different size than the others.

I needed to talk to Robin.

Gabe and Glenda went to bed early. Although it was close to nine o'clock, the sky was still light, and pink-and-gold-streaked clouds stretched above the hills to the west.

Glenda suggested, "You might like to watch television until you're sleepy, Julie. Just keep the volume low."

"Thanks," I said, "but I'd rather spend some time online."

I turned off the lights in the living room and was crossing it, headed for Uncle Gabe's office, when a small flash of light from outside caught my attention.

"What was that?" I said aloud.

As I walked toward the windows, the flash of light came again. It was off to the side of the house, near the carport. Maybe it was an outside light with a bad connection. Maybe it came from one of the cars.

No matter what had caused the flash, it needed to be checked out.

I walked out the front door, glad it was not dark enough to keep me from seeing my way, and walked to the carport. I had no sooner reached the foot of the observatory stairs than a dark shadow unfolded from under them and stepped out. The beam from the flashlight in the man's hand shone first on me, then on the ground.

I jumped back, yelling, "Who are you? What are you doing here?"

"I didn't mean to startle you," the man said. He was tall and lean with broad shoulders. His deep blue eyes were narrowed like crevasses in the craggy Sierra Madres, his skin as sun-browned and weathered as earth. "I'm Cal Grant, the foreman of Rancho del Oro."

My heart was still pounding loudly. I tried to calm down and said, "My aunt and uncle don't know you're here. They've already gone to bed."

"I didn't come to see them," he said. "And I didn't mean to disturb anybody. After I talked to the deputy I came to see what you was fussin' about. Foster was right. There's nothin' there."

"Nail holes are there," I said.

"Right. A passel of 'em, up and down the stairs."

"That's not what I meant. There are two holes near—"

"It's gettin' dark," he interrupted, and shined his flashlight beam along the walk to the house. "Better get inside while you can still see where you're goin' or you might trip and fall."

I realized there was no point in trying to get to know Cal Grant or asking him any questions about the ranch and the people who lived and worked there. He wasn't the least bit friendly. Also, I didn't like it that he had come to the house without letting Gabe and Glenda know he was there. I walked back to the front door and, after I stepped inside, made sure it was securely locked.

I went straight to Gabe's study, settled into his comfortable office chair, and turned on my laptop.

The familiar voice told me, "You've got mail."

But I saw from my buddy list that Robin was already online, so I sent a message her way:

Jul59: Robin, glad you're here. I need to talk.
Robinor: Hi, Jul. What's up?
Jul59: I told Uncle Gabe about the nail holes. He called a deputy who looked and said they were just holes Gabe had made when he built the stairs.
Robinor: That's good news.
Jul59: No. I mean, I don't believe the deputy. He showed me other nail holes, but they were from larger nails. The two holes I found were tiny, from very small nails. Gabe told me he had only used the larger nails.
Robinor: Have you found out anything else?
Jul59: No. Robin, I'm scared. I think someone did cause Gabe's fall. And I think he might try again. But I don't know what to do.
Robinor: Me either.
Jul59: You're the one who reads mysteries. Shouldn't I look for some kind of clues?
Robinor: The nail holes are clues. They tell us that the person who caused the fall is someone who

either lives or works on the ranch. He's someone who could put those nails in the steps without anyone noticing.

Jul59: Then what?

Robinor: I don't know. You'll figure it out. We're driving to Santa Barbara tomorrow and won't be back until Friday evening. I'll get in touch when we're home again.

I typed in **Thanks. Bye** and leaned back in Gabe's chair, more frustrated than ever, as I tried to think.

Tomorrow I'll try to work it out, I told myself with a long sigh. Tonight I needed to answer my e-mail.

There was another note from Mom, complaining that I had been gone three whole days and hadn't told her anything in my only e-mail to her. She added:

Did you remember to bring your sunscreen with you? Even from his hospital bed, your uncle Richard's thoughts were about you. He sent word to remind you to wear your sunscreen every time you go out, and to be aware that the two-hour time difference will take about a week to get used to, so don't overdo. Get lots of rest and listen to your body.

"I could hear my body a lot more clearly if people would stop telling me what to do!" I muttered to myself, but I only wrote **Everything's fine. Love, Julie.**

I wished I had asked Robin if the swim team was doing any better, but in a way I was glad she hadn't told me. It hurt too much that I wasn't taking part. I was still angry with my family for directing my life without giving me a chance to make up my own mind.

Two of my friends wrote "How I'm spending my summer vacation" letters, but since they were mostly about guys they had met, I just gritted my teeth and sent short answers that sounded as if I were having just as good a time. Who would be interested in the elderly people I was meeting? Nobody.

I jumped as a snap like a twig breaking came from just outside the window. I stared at the open shutters and saw nothing but the deep blackness outside. Something or someone was out there. I could feel it. My hands grew clammy, and it was hard to breathe as I listened intently for another sound of movement, but the night was silent.

It's only a cow, I told myself. Calm down. Don't be so ready to be scared.

I turned back to my laptop and the e-mail I'd received from Ellie, one of my friends on the swim team. I clicked on **Reply** and began typing:

Let me know the scores you make at each of the meets. I wish I could

I jumped again as just under the window came a dull thump, as if someone had bumped the outside wall. I stiffened, not daring to look up. Was someone outside the window, looking in? Although my legs were trembling, I knew I had to investigate. I couldn't just sit there and allow myself to be watched, not even by a cow.

I shut off my laptop, then stood up slowly and stretched. Forcing myself to remain calm, I slowly sauntered out of the study. When I was in the hallway, out of the window's range of vision, I ran to the kitchen door and silently opened it.

Slipping through, I made my way around to the back of the house. Golden strips of light beamed through the open shutters onto the ground under the study window.

No one was there.

I glanced to each side and saw only the empty clearing with the tangled vines and trees of the forest massing beyond. There was no sign that cattle had been there, so I couldn't blame a cow for making the noises that had frightened me.

I didn't like being alone in the darkness, so I hurried to the kitchen door and reached for the handle. I tugged, expecting it to open, and was shocked when it didn't budge. The door was locked.

I hadn't locked it. I knew I hadn't. It was the kind of knob with a center button you had to push in and turn. They were so easy for intruders to open with a credit card that everyone in Santa Monica had installed dead bolts for better protection. If I just had a credit card to push the lock back . . . but I didn't.

Behind me, I heard the rustle of bushes. Whirling, I pressed my back against the door. Opposite me, at the edge of the clearing, I could sense movement. Shadowy movement I was barely able to make out. Whatever was there was well hidden by the dark night.

But I was out here with it.

Turning, I pounded on the door, yelling in panic, "Aunt Glenda! Help me! Let me in!"

Chapter Six

I THOUGHT I HEARD SOMEONE COMING CLOSER AND CLOSER. I could feel eyes boring into my back. I yelled and pounded all the harder, and when the door suddenly swung open, I stumbled and fell into the kitchen. "Shut the door! Hurry!" I shouted.

Glenda tugged on my arm, pulling me to my feet. "Julie!" she cried. "What happened? What's the matter?"

"Somebody locked me out of the house," I said. "Then he came after me."

I turned and saw that the door was still open. Glenda had stepped to the sill and was peering outside. "No one is there," she said.

"He was," I said, leaning against her and trying to make out shapes in the darkness. "I'm sure of it."

A deer stepped from the shadows of the trees into the clearing, his eyes reflecting the kitchen's light, and Glenda gave a relieved sigh. "There you are," she said. "What you saw and heard was only a deer. You accidentally locked the door and didn't realize it."

Glenda shut the door and turned the button in the knob. "It's a good thing Gabe took those pills the doctor gave him," she said. "He's sleeping through all the racket. Otherwise, he'd be banging around in here with his crutches, demanding I call the deputy."

"I'm sorry," I said, trying to explain. "I was afraid, and I couldn't get back into the house."

She led me to the kitchen table. "I'm going to heat some milk for you," she said. "It will help you relax."

She poured milk into a pan and put it on the stove. Then she gave me her full attention and said, "Tell me what happened, right from the beginning."

I did, and she said, "You only *thought* someone was out there. You saw the deer. That's all it was. I told you, we have animals that make night noises. Rabbits . . . squirrels . . . remember?"

"An animal didn't lock me out of the house."

Glenda glanced toward the door as she answered, "You said that someone was outside, not *inside*, where he could lock the door." She poured the steaming milk into a mug, brought it to me, then sat in a chair directly across the table.

"Trying to make your way outside at night would make anyone nervous," she told me. "And it would be easy to accidentally turn the lock in the knob without realizing it. It's loose. It could turn easily in your hand without your noticing."

She reached across the table and gripped my hands. "This is all Gabe's fault. His trying to blame someone for his fall, and making such a big deal about those foolish nail holes, has only fed your imagination. I'm going to tell Gabe that he's positively not to say another word about being tripped on the stairs, and you're not going to even think about it. It's over and done with. Understand?"

"Yes," I answered reluctantly. I couldn't prove to myself one way or another that the door had locked accidentally, so it wouldn't help to argue about it. What Glenda had said made sense. I had to admit she was probably right.

"Good," Glenda said, and gave my hands a final pat. "You are not in danger. I'd never want that. Gabe and I are fine, too. Now drink your milk, and let's both be off to bed."

I dutifully went to my room, but I couldn't sleep. I kicked off my blanket and lay with my eyes wide open, listening . . . waiting . . . for what? I didn't know. The silence of the night was a thick black sludge, slowly creeping into every corner of the room. At some point, it closed around me, covering me, and I slept.

The morning sun, poking through the blinds in golden stripes, woke me, and I was surprised to see that it was close to eight-thirty. I hurried to dress. Ashley had said she'd come this morning, and I hoped she wasn't already waiting for me.

I rushed into the kitchen so fast I tripped over a pair of long, jean-clad legs that stuck out from under the kitchen sink. I went sprawling. "Ouch!" I cried.

"Ouch!" echoed a voice from under the sink.

I sat up as the owner of the legs squirmed out from under the sink and faced me.

"I'm sorry. I hope I didn't hurt you," I said to one of the best-looking guys I'd ever seen. His eyes were almost as dark as his hair, and they widened with surprise as he looked at me.

"I'm not hurt. Are you?" he asked.

I stopped rubbing my knee. "I'm okay," I said. "I just didn't expect you to be there."

A wide smile spread across his face. "And I didn't expect you to drop into my lap."

I suddenly realized that my legs were still draped across his, and I scrambled back, sitting cross-legged. I said, "We'd better start over. I'm Julie Hollister. Gabe and Glenda Hollister are my dad's uncle and aunt. I'm here to visit them for the summer."

"And I'm Luis Garcia," he answered. "I'm here to fix the drain under the sink."

We both laughed.

I spoke first. "Aunt Glenda told me about you. She said you're in high school."

"For one more year," Luis told me. "Then I plan to go to Texas A&M. Because I'm number two in my class, I've got a good chance for early admission and a scholarship."

"That's great," I said. "You sound pretty organized. What are you going to major in? I bet you know already."

"Computer science. Where the money is. A&M has a good program." He grinned and shrugged and I noticed how broad his shoulders were. "I love anything to do with computers. My mom complains that I spend too much time with them."

Glenda came into the kitchen just then and stared down at us. "My goodness, Julie," she said. "Are you helping Luis?"

"Not exactly," I answered.

"She will," Luis said. "If she'll hand me that pipe wrench over there."

As I did, he smiled up at Glenda and said, "I'll tighten the U-joint and the job will be finished. I cleaned it out, and you should have no more trouble. I've got those bedding plants you wanted in my truck. I'll plant them where you showed me."

I climbed to my feet and kept chatting with Luis while he washed his hands and Glenda wrote out a check for him. After he'd left, I took a good look at Glenda. There were dark circles under her eyes, and the skin around her cheeks sagged. Guilt swept over me. I'd been sent here to *help* Aunt Glenda, not make life more difficult for her.

"I'm sorry I frightened you last night," I said. "You were right. No one was outside. I must have let my imagination go wild."

My aunt put an arm around my shoulders. "Don't blame yourself. I hadn't gone to sleep yet when you called for help. I'd been thinking . . . and there were those night sounds. . . . Living out here is nothing like living in the city with people close by. It's difficult to get used to at first."

I wasn't convinced she had ever become used to it. Even after living here well over a year, neither Glenda nor her friends seemed to have grown used to life on Rancho del Oro. I made a quick breakfast and had no sooner finished gulping it down than Ashley knocked at the back door.

Wiping my hands on my shorts, I pulled open the door. "Hi," I said. "Come on in. Did you bring your swimsuit?"

She nodded and held up a thin plastic bag. Inside I could see something blue with a price tag attached. She must have bought a new suit after I asked her to go swimming. I smiled and said, "Let's put on our suits and go down to the pool now, before it gets too hot. I'll show you where the bathroom is so you can change." I hoped she knew how to swim. I pulled on my team's dark blue one-piece suit, hoping I could still be part of this summer's competition. Stepping into my flip-flops and taking Glenda's car keys from the key board in the kitchen, I waited for Ashley.

When she came into the kitchen, a T-shirt over her suit, I handed her the tube of sunscreen and led her out the front door, heading toward the carport.

If I'd been moving any faster, I might have tripped over Luis again. He was on his knees, carefully planting yellow and orange marigolds next to the front of the house.

"Let's hope the cows don't like the taste or smell of marigolds," he said.

"Snails do," Ashley said. It was a simple statement, but she made it sound as if Luis didn't know what he was doing.

I looked from Luis to Ashley and back again. "Do you two know each other?" I asked.

"Sure," Luis said. He didn't look in Ashley's direction, but he gave me a big smile as he added, "We already said hello when Ashley's grandmother dropped her off."

Ashley didn't say anything. The tension in their attitude toward each other was making me uncomfortable, so I said, "We'll see you later, Luis," and walked to the car.

Once we were in the car and I had backed into the road, I said to Ashley, "When I first got here I thought I was going to be living with a lot of elderly people, so it's great to know that I'll get to spend time with you and Luis."

I thought that would get Ashley to open up, but she didn't say a word, so I tried again to make conversation. "Have you known Luis for very long?"

"Yes," she said.

"He seems like a nice guy."

She didn't answer.

It was obvious that our conversation wasn't going anywhere as long as it concerned Luis. Even though I was curious, I couldn't be nosy and ask why she didn't like him, so I changed the subject. "Do you know how to swim?" I asked.

"Yes," Ashley said. "I've taken swimming the last three semesters, and I made the school's team." For the first time she smiled. "My best stroke is the butterfly. When we get to the pool, I'll race you."

I had a surprise coming. I lost the first race to Ashley because I thought she couldn't possibly beat my record. In the next race I tried as hard as if I were in a meet with my own team. I managed to come in first, but it was tight.

I leaned on the edge of the pool as I struggled to catch my breath. "You're good," I said.

She rested her head against the tile edge and smiled. She was breathing almost as hard as I was, but she managed to say, "Thanks. You are too. Where do you swim?"

"Our subdivision has a swim club," I told her. Suddenly, I could picture so vividly the members of our team racing cleanly through the water that I spoke out in anguish. "We were going for the championship this year. I know we would have made it, but my parents decided it wasn't important that I take part. But it was. It was to me. I hate having so many people make decisions that affect me, just because they're family, and not being able to decide things by myself."

Ashley gave me a strange quick look, then curled into a surface dive. I watched her swim away underwater, then reappear at the opposite end of the pool.

I found it hard to understand Ashley. Sometimes she seemed friendly, sometimes she didn't—and I didn't know why. She made it clear that she didn't like Luis, and at times she didn't seem to like me. Maybe it was just that she was shy, but for some reason her actions seemed defensive.

I climbed out of the pool and lay on one of the beach chairs, letting the sun blot the water from my back. In a few minutes, Ashley stretched out in the chair next to me. She didn't speak, and I was trying to decide if I should start another conversation when the Hunk arrived.

He didn't say hello. He just flexed his bronzed muscles and said, "I hope you kids aren't going back in the pool for a while. I'm going to vacuum it."

Kids! What a jerk. I flipped over to take a good look at him. Up close I could see leathery lines in his face and realized that he was probably close to thirty. I thought of Uncle Gabe's telescope and how I had trained it on the pool and on some of the surrounding houses. The Jerk/Hunk had looked much better at a distance.

He poked his vacuum wand down to the bottom of the pool. Then, as though he knew I was sizing him up, he looked directly at me. "You ever live on ranch country before?" he asked me.

"No," I answered.

"It takes getting used to," he said. "Especially at night when it's easy to get lost. Don't go out in the dark again by your lonesome."

I sat up, alert. "What are you talking about?"

"Last night I heard you yelling for help all the way down here."

"Here? The pool isn't open at night."

"Sometimes I bunk on the couch in the office."

I examined him suspiciously. "How did you know it was me?"

"Direction. It had to be the Hollister house."

"If you heard me yelling for help, why didn't you come?" I asked.

His shoulders rippled in a shrug. "While I was thinking on it, you stopped."

Angry now, I persisted. "What if I stopped because I'd been hurt?"

"You weren't hurt," he said. "Mrs. Hollister opened the door and let you back in the house."

"How'd you know that?"

Again he shrugged. "Figures. She was there, wasn't she?"

He moved away, intent on examining the bottom of the pool, while I tried to sort through what he'd said. Was he really guessing correctly at what had happened, or did he know what had happened because he had been there in the darkness? Had I been right? What if this guy had watched me through the unshuttered windows as I worked in Gabe's office? Had he opened the back door to reach inside and turn the lock in the doorknob and then hidden at the edge of the woods?

I was lobbing questions to myself at a fast clip until one popped up that stopped me cold. *What reason could he have had for being at the house?* I couldn't see any possible connection between this pool guy and Uncle Gabe.

Ashley spoke, startling me so much that I jumped. "What was Damien talking about?"

"That's his name? Damien?" I blurted out. He looked as though his name should be Rocky or Tony, not Damien.

"Yes. Damien Fitch. I told you. He lives in the trailer next to Gran's and he drives that scratched-up black sedan we parked next to. So? Tell me. Why were you yelling for help last night?"

I told her most of the story, mentioning that I must have accidentally locked the door as I went out, then had panicked when I couldn't get back inside. I expected her to laugh, but she didn't.

"It *is* scary up here after dark," she said. "I don't blame you for being frightened. *I* would have been."

I was grateful for Ashley's support. I guess I could have told her my suspicions that someone actually had reached in and locked that door. However, something held me back. Maybe because I just didn't know Ashley well enough. Maybe because I still didn't understand her.

Glenda and Gabe seemed to. During the afternoon,

while the four of us played Chinese checkers, Gabe teased Ashley and made her laugh. Glenda and Ashley found they had read the same biography and practically got into a Great Books discussion. To my surprise, I realized that Glenda and Gabe seemed to know more about Ashley than they did about me.

When Millie Lee drove by to pick up Ashley, Gabe and Glenda appeared to be as sorry to see her go as I was.

"Come back tomorrow," I said.

"I will, if it's okay with Gran," Ashley promised.

"Lovely girl," Glenda said as she waved at the departing car. "I'm sorry her family . . ." Her words drifted away, but I remembered what she had told me.

That evening, when I was alone at dinner with Gabe and Glenda, I asked, "Do you know much about Damien Fitch?"

"Who's Damien Fitch?" Gabe asked, his energies focused on the steaming hot, once-frozen lasagna he was eating.

"He's the lifeguard at your pool," I said.

"Never heard of him," Gabe said. He took a large bite.

"We're just not much for swimming," Glenda apologized. "I do remember him, though. He came to the house in early May with a membership form to be signed if we wanted to use the swimming pool. He seemed like a pleasant young man. We had a nice chat while he drank his coffee."

"You invited him in?" I asked.

"Why, yes," she answered. "He asked for a drink of water, and I offered iced tea, but he preferred coffee."

She gave me a questioning look and added, "We're hospitable in Texas, Julie."

Gabe looked up from his plate and asked, "What do you want us to know about him?"

"Nothing, really," I answered, feeling stupid because there was no way I could come up with a sensible answer. "I just wondered if you knew him."

"We chatted about all sorts of things," Glenda said. "I remember he asked about the Dime Box, and I told him its story."

Gabe scraped the last bite of lasagna from his plate, put it in his mouth, and asked, "By the way, does anybody know where my Dime Box is now?"

I glanced toward the kitchen counter near the back door. "It's over—" I stopped short. "If you mean that ceramic bank with the name 'Dime Box' on its roof, I was going to say it's on the counter where you usually keep it, but now it's not."

"Somebody moved it," Gabe complained.

"It was probably you," Glenda said. "You're always moving it around from the kitchen to your study or taking it into the living room to show it off when someone comes visiting. I'm sure everyone in Rancho del Oro has seen that bank."

I broke in. "It looks like a bank building, but why is it named Dime Box?"

Gabe grinned. "I got it thirty or forty years ago in Dime Box, Texas. Yep, there's really a town with that name. That old bank is probably a collector's item by this time, and I'm guessing it must hold a good hundred dollars' worth of dimes."

"It's heavy enough," Glenda remarked.

"Will you look for it?" Gabe asked. "It's got to be somewhere around the house."

Glenda and I both agreed to look, and later we did, but we couldn't find the bank. Glenda wasn't worried about its disappearance. "Gabe just laid it down in some odd place he's forgotten about," she said. "Sooner or later it will show up."

I remembered the conversation at Mrs. Barrow's luncheon about people mislaying things. My face must have shown what I was thinking, because Glenda said, "His age has nothing to do with the Dime Box being missing. It's just the problem of living in a new place and getting used to new things. Why, my goodness, that bank may be hidden in the same place as my amethyst bracelet. Someplace safe. New cubbyholes . . ."

Glenda and Gabe had lived here well over a year. Their house wasn't exactly new. I couldn't help being puzzled by the missing bank. I had noticed the Dime Box on the counter on Monday morning, while I ate breakfast, but I couldn't remember when I had last seen it there.

"Where is your amethyst bracelet?" I asked Glenda.

She started, then looked down, pink flooding her cheeks. "I wish I knew," she said.

"You've lost it?"

"No. Only misplaced it," she answered. "I remember putting it in a place where no one could find it. At least, I think I did. I meant to do so." She looked up at me and shrugged. "It's somewhere in this house."

"Was the Dime Box near the back door last night?" I quietly asked Glenda when we were out of Gabe's hearing.

"I don't think so," she said, but I wondered if she was right.

The next day, aside from time spent with Ashley, I helped Glenda with odd jobs—like reorganizing everything in the linen closet. I played endless games of gin rummy with Glenda and Gabe, and I double-checked Glenda, who made sure Gabe took all his medications by making a chart and using a kitchen timer.

However, in the late evening, when the house seemed a small, brightly lit oasis in a desert of blackness, I couldn't help feeling that someone was out there watching us. I knew I must be wrong and only imagining things, but in that dark hole of a ranch, when the silence grew menacing, I kept listening intently for something to break the pattern. When it did, when there was a rustle outside, or the snap of a twig, or the thud of what might be a footfall, I jumped, holding my breath.

It didn't help that Glenda was just as nervous as I was. We didn't speak about it, but I could tell we felt the same. We both seemed to be waiting for what would happen next.

Chapter Seven

WHEN MILLIE LEE ARRIVED ON FRIDAY MORNING TO CLEAN, Ashley wasn't with her.

Millie Lee, busy pulling cleaning supplies from the top shelf of the pantry, didn't look at me. "Ashley said I should tell you she was busy this mornin'," Millie Lee said. Then, lowering her voice, as though she were talking to herself, she added, "That girl's just as aggravatin' as her mother."

The way Millie Lee was grumping around, I began to suspect that she and Ashley had had a major disagreement. I was glad I wasn't the one Ashley was avoiding.

Because Ashley didn't talk much when we were together, I'd hunt for something to chat about. Last time I'd opened up about my brother Hayden, who at ten was a real pest, and I'd told a funny story about my sister, Bitsy, who was probably the most spoiled four-year-old in the world. And I hadn't left out my six-year-old brother, Trevor, who had perfected the art of pouting in a big way.

Ashley hadn't laughed or groaned at my stories or

come back with a family story of her own, as any other girl I knew would do. She'd abruptly told me she had to meet her grandmother, and she'd walked away.

I said to Millie Lee, "Please tell Ashley I hope she comes tomorrow."

Millie Lee just grunted as she began unloading the dishwasher. I took that as a yes.

As I helped put dishes in the cupboard, I tried making conversation. "Ashley told me that Damien Fitch, the lifeguard, lives next door to you."

Millie Lee turned to me, rolling her eyes. "Don't go gettin' any ideas about Damien just 'cause he's so good-lookin'. For one thing, he's much too old for you."

Startled, I giggled, and she scowled. "That's not a joke," she said.

"I'm not interested in Damien," I assured her. "I guess that's why I laughed. The idea struck me funny."

"It's not," she said. "Besides . . ."

I waited, but she was silent.

"Besides what?" I finally asked.

"Never you mind," she said. "That's all you need to know about Damien."

What she had said made me even more curious, but I knew I wouldn't get any answers from her. She picked up a fistful of rags and a can of cleanser and headed down the hall toward the bathrooms, and I walked to the den to play cards with Glenda and Gabe.

What had Millie Lee meant when she'd said "Besides" and didn't finish? I wondered.

"Wake up and pay attention, Julie," Gabe said. "It's your turn."

"Sorry," I told him. I pushed all thoughts of Damien out of my mind and concentrated on the card game.

A short while later, as we tallied the scores from the first game, Gabe asked, "Julie, would you mind getting my reading glasses? I really don't need them—my eyes are as good as they ever were—but the marks on these cards seem to be getting smaller."

I returned Glenda's smile. "Sure, Uncle Gabe. Where did you leave them?"

"Probably in the bedroom," he said. "Or maybe in my study."

"You haven't been in your study," Glenda told him.

I got up quickly. "Wherever they are, I'll find them," I said, and headed in the direction of Gabe's study, just to satisfy him.

As I entered the room, Millie Lee slapped down the top of my laptop and took a step backward, her eyes wide. "You scared me, poppin' in like that," she said. Then she quickly recovered, adding, "You got a nice little computer. I just had to take a look at it."

All Millie Lee was doing was looking. I shouldn't mind. "Would you like me to show you some of its special features?" I asked her.

"Maybe some other time," she answered. "Right now I've got work to finish, and you've got things to do."

"Okay," I said. "I'm looking for Uncle Gabe's glasses."

"On top of the dresser in his bedroom," she told me, and began dusting the top of his desk.

I found the glasses right away, and the game went on,

but I couldn't help wondering how much of my computer Millie Lee had investigated. My Internet password was automatically stored, so anyone could have gone into my e-mail. But surely there'd be no reason for her to do that.

"Julie, pay attention," Gabe said impatiently. "I just ginned. How many points do you owe me?"

"Too many," I said. I began to count, putting Millie Lee and my laptop out of my mind.

I was lonesome for someone my own age to talk to, so I was glad when Luis arrived in the early evening.

I brought him some iced tea, which Uncle Gabe called the national drink of Texas, and two of the cookies from the package we'd served for dessert after supper. We sat on the front steps to talk.

It was a lot easier to talk with Luis than it was with Ashley.

Once I'd told him I had brought my laptop, Luis talked on and on about computers, describing programs I hadn't even known existed. As the trees cast long, ragged strips of shade across our porch, he began describing the way computer graphics were used in major movies. "I'm going to do that someday," he said. "Computers are going to make me rich.

"It's great to imagine all the things I can someday do with computers," he added, "and with my life—if I only make the right moves."

I was afraid to ask what he meant. It might mean another long explanation. So I changed the subject. "I haven't been to the stables yet, and I love to ride. Come horseback riding with me," I said.

For an instant Luis looked surprised. Then he said, "Not yet. Julie, you forget. I'm a repairman. I'm a gardener."

"What difference does that make?" I asked.

"It makes a difference to people who own private stables," he said quietly.

"It doesn't to me."

"You're just a guest here. You can't change the rules."

Stubbornly, I said, "I don't believe anyone wrote rules that would keep you out."

"Someday I'll make my own rules and decide for myself who gets left out."

"Why should *anyone* be left out?" I demanded, ready for an argument.

But Luis raised his glass of tea in salute and smiled. "It's good just being here with you," he said. He drained his glass and said firmly, "Now I must go back to work."

It was clear that I'd been dismissed, so I wandered back into the house. Gabe had gone to sleep in his chair, his magazine spread across his lap, and Glenda sat at the kitchen table, working on a crossword puzzle. The more I thought about going riding, the more it appealed to me. I'd ridden before and knew how to handle a horse. There was no reason I couldn't ride by myself.

"Is it all right if I drive down to the stables?" I asked Glenda.

"Um-hmm," she murmured without looking up.

I took the car keys and drove to the stables. The groom saddled a horse for me and held it while I mounted. "It's getting late," he said. "Follow the trails.

Don't stay out too long. Be sure you bring Duffy back before dark."

Duffy was broad, a little bit overweight, and obviously lazy. He plodded along the trail, snorting in disgust when I tried to guide him or get him to move a little faster. In many places the trail paralleled the road, and we passed a few homes I hadn't seen before. Although the houses were large, two even quite elegant, there were no lawns or gardens and nothing of the beauty women try to give their homes. Along the trail I saw no one. The loneliness, the deep silence of the ranch depressed me.

I lost all sense of time, and when the trail passed through a grove of trees, I realized with a start that the sun was going down and darkness was closing in quickly.

I turned Duffy in the direction of the stables. I hoped he'd pick up speed, heading toward home, but instead he raised his head, eyes wide, shying from the nearby trees on our left.

As I soothed him, firmly gripping the reins, I glanced over to see what had spooked him. Inside the dim grove, I could barely make out the shape of another horse and rider—someone who seemed to want to stay out of sight.

My heart began to thump loudly, and my good sense skittered right out of my head. With a yell of fright, I dug my heels into Duffy, who surprisingly shifted into overdrive and began to run.

I could hear the other horse behind me. I bent low, urging Duffy to run faster, but the other horse was upon us. His rider reached out, roughly smashing against my shoulder as he grabbed the reins from my hands. He quickly brought Duffy to a stop.

"You have to be a fool to race a horse in the dark!" he exclaimed.

I looked up at Cal Grant and rubbed my shoulder. "You didn't need to be so rough."

The anger in his voice didn't lessen. "You could have injured both your horse and yourself."

"I had to run! You were hiding from me! You scared me!" I snapped back at him. "What were you doing there?"

Cal handed me the reins and drew his own horse back without answering. He wheeled his horse around and rode into the darkness.

I urged Duffy on, and he trotted directly to the stables, where the groom gave me another scolding for coming back so late.

Shaken, I drove home to Glenda and Gabe.

Glenda met me at the door, and she was obviously upset. Her hands shook as she reached for me and pulled me inside the house.

"I'm sorry I'm so late," I began, but she brushed my apology aside.

"Eugene Barrow died a short time ago," she said.

"Ann Barrow's husband? What happened?" I asked. Glenda led me to the sofa, and we sat together. Gabe, a worried frown on his face, watched us from his reclining chair.

"All I heard from Mabel, when she called me, was that they're guessing that Eugene mistakenly took too much of his heart medication. The bottle was lying on the floor, nearly empty. Even a normal dose made him dizzy if he stood up too suddenly. A stronger dose would have had a worse effect."

"His medication killed him?" I asked.

"Oh, no, Julie. It just made him dizzy, so it's no wonder that he fell."

A shiver ran up my backbone. A third husband falling—two of them to their deaths? What was going on?

Glenda continued. "He struck his head on the ledge of the stone fireplace. Just think, he built that fireplace himself two years ago when he and Ann came here to live."

"I'm so sorry it happened," I said. "Was Mrs. Barrow with him when he fell?"

Sighing, Glenda answered, "Ann wasn't home. She had gone to play bridge at the clubhouse, as she and Eugene have done every Friday night. He complained that he didn't feel like going, so this time she went without him. That makes it even more terrible for her. She blames herself. She said she should have been with Eugene, supervising his medication, but Mabel told me what she had told Ann—that Eugene has been relatively healthy and has never needed supervision before."

Glenda clutched my hands, pleading, "Julie, will you drive me to see Ann Barrow? I want to pay my respects and bring a pound cake I've got in the freezer."

I cleaned up in a hurry and was dressed and ready to leave by the time Glenda's cake was on a plate.

"Are you sure you'll be all right by yourself for a little while? We won't be long," she told Gabe.

I could hear the worry in her voice. I was a little worried too. I felt torn in two directions, but Glenda was in no state to drive herself.

"I'll be fine," Gabe answered.

"Should I try to get hold of Millie Lee? Maybe she'd be free to sit with you."

Gabe's eyebrows ran together like a shaggy caterpillar and he thundered, "You think I need a babysitter? At my age?"

"I just—"

"I'll be all right by myself! Now go!"

Although Glenda had told me they rarely locked the outside doors, since they felt so well protected on the ranch, I noticed that she carefully locked the back and front doors as we left the house.

Quite a few people were crowded into the Barrows' living room when we arrived. Glenda hugged Mrs. Barrow tightly and they both cried a little as we told her how sorry we were about her husband's sudden death.

I recognized the women who had been at the luncheon, and I was introduced to a number of husbands. Casseroles, salads, platters of cheese and sliced ham, and plates of cookies and cakes filled the dining room table, and people were helping themselves to coffee from a large urn at one end of the sideboard.

I said hello to Millie Lee, who had come to help out in the kitchen, and was glad to see that Ashley was with her.

"I was hoping you'd come to see me yesterday or today," I told Ashley.

She watched her grandmother pull the wrap from a plate of brownies and head with the plate toward the dining room before she answered. "Gran took on a new job yesterday. She had a spot open after Mrs. Crouch left so she gave it to the Hodges. It's extra work at first, so I went with her to help her."

Ashley didn't give an excuse for not coming with her grandmother to our house that morning, and I didn't push it. I just grinned and said, "I'd love another chance to beat you—backstroke or butterfly."

She smiled in return. "How about Monday?"

"You're on," I said. Then I got a sudden idea. "Aunt Glenda told me she'll only be here a short time because she doesn't want to leave Uncle Gabe alone for long. Why don't you come back to their house with me, and we'll see what Gabe's telescope can do with the stars."

Ashley's eyes lit up, but she had no chance to answer.

Millie Lee, returning to the kitchen, spoke for her. "That would be nice," she said. "Ashley, you go with the Hollisters when they leave, and I'll pick you up at their house about ten or ten-thirty."

"Won't you need me to help you?" Ashley asked.

Shaking her head, Millie Lee said, "I'm used to doin' just fine without you. There's not that much work here besides puttin' out the food people bring. Then, after they all leave, makin' sure that what needs keepin' cold gets put in the refrigerator."

"I'll help you until the Hollisters leave," Ashley insisted. She picked up a plate of bite-sized sandwiches and carried it toward the dining room.

I said, "See you in a few minutes," then wandered

back to the living room. I found a seat near the fireplace—an area everyone seemed to be avoiding. I couldn't help looking at the brick ledge around the fireplace, where Mr. Barrow had fallen and hit his head. There was no way of telling what had happened. The bricks must have been scrubbed clean. I glanced next at the nearby table where I'd seen the company paperweight that meant so much to Mrs. Barrow and was surprised to see that the paperweight wasn't there.

She's showing it to someone, I thought, but for some reason I had to make sure. I got up and edged over to where Mrs. Barrow was standing, being comforted by some of her friends.

"I'll be going home—back to Houston—soon as I can sell this house," she was saying. Her smile wobbled, and I could hear a strange note of eagerness in her voice. "My son and his family live there, you know. Three darling boys and one girl. I just can't see enough of them. Annabelle's six, just the right age to begin going with her grandmother to the symphony's First Concert programs for children."

Everyone in the group began telling grandchildren stories, and I left the group. Mrs. Barrow wasn't holding the paperweight, and it wasn't on the table near her. I slowly circled the living room, looking in every possible spot, and convinced myself that the paperweight was no longer in the living room.

No one was paying any attention to me, so I slipped out of the room and made a quick trip through the two large bedrooms and the bathrooms. No sign of the paperweight. Why was it missing? It couldn't have meant anything to anyone but the Barrows. I wondered if Mrs. Barrow had already packed it away.

I saw her enter a bathroom, so I waited for her. The moment she stepped back into the hall, I stopped her. "I was looking for your paperweight," I said.

"Paperweight?" She looked puzzled for a moment. Then she said, "Oh, the company paperweight. It should be where I always keep it, on the table by the fireplace."

She didn't know that her paperweight was missing. So of course she wouldn't know who had taken it.

I jumped as someone rested a hand on my shoulder. Turning quickly, I saw that it was Millie Lee.

"Julie," she said, "your aunt's lookin' for you. She said it's time to get home to make sure your uncle takes his medicine."

Glenda and I said our goodbyes to Mrs. Barrow and to some of the others. Ashley joined us, and we drove home.

As we came in the door, Uncle Gabe pushed himself upright in his chair, rubbed his eyes, and tried to pretend he hadn't fallen asleep.

After he had greeted Ashley, I asked, "May we please use your observatory, Uncle Gabe? It's a clear night, and we'd love to try your telescope."

He beamed with pleasure. "I wish I could be with you. The moment this old ankle is healed . . ."

I took the key from the board in the kitchen and a flashlight from the drawer Glenda had shown me. Then I led Ashley down the path from the front door to the stairs to the observatory. I kept my eyes straight ahead.

I was surprised when Ashley said, "It's so spooky out here. At least in the trailer park we have plenty of light."

Our weight on the wooden steps caused pops and creaks that seemed really loud. Ashley pressed close to me as I inserted the key into the lock and pushed the door open.

Once inside, with the lights on and the door firmly closed, we both relaxed. Ashley leaned against the door and giggled. "Don't mind me," she said. "When I was little I thought a monster lived under my bed."

I laughed, then rested my hand on the gleaming brass telescope. "Let's see what this beautiful thing can show us," I said. "You first."

We raised the blinds on all the windows, turned off the lights, and took turns with the telescope. It must have been top of the line, because the clarity was wonderful. Ashley knew more about astronomy than I did, so she pointed out a couple of constellations that were new to me. At least, thanks to my fifth-grade teacher, who had given me my first taste of astronomy, I could find the Big and Little Dippers and Orion's belt.

All too soon, we saw the headlights from Millie Lee's car sweep up the hill and across our driveway.

Ashley quickly began helping me lower the blinds and put the telescope back in place. "This was great," she said. "I'm glad I came. Thanks for inviting me."

She really was glad. I could tell. Maybe she was finally warming up to me.

I locked up, said goodbye to Ashley, and waved to Millie Lee. As I went into the house, Glenda got up from her chair and kissed me good night.

"Gabe's already in bed," she said, "and that's where I'm going too."

I wasn't ready for bed. I sat at my laptop in Gabe's office, intending to e-mail Robin. It was Friday night, and she should have returned home. But I didn't have to e-mail. Her name popped up on my buddy list in the upper corner of my screen, so I knew she was home and online, probably checking her e-mail. I went into an instant message.

> **Jul59:** Hi, Robin. How was Santa Barbara?
> **Robinor:** Great, as always. UK?
> **Jul59:** K, I guess. But one of the other men who lives on the ranch died in a fall.
> **Robinor:** What! Tell me everything. Every detail.

I did, and even though it didn't seem to be important, I told her about the missing paperweight.

> **Robinor:** Paperweight? Wow! I've read two mysteries in which a paperweight was the murder weapon.
> **Jul59:** Mr. Barrow's death wasn't a murder. The deputy was satisfied that Mr. Barrow fell and hit his head on the corner of the stone fireplace.
> **Robinor:** What did the medical examiner rule?
> **Jul59:** What medical examiner?
> **Robinor:** If there's any suspicion of murder, then the medical examiner has to be called in. The body can't be released to the family until the m.e. says so.
> **Jul59:** Are you sure?
> **Robinor:** Of course I'm sure. It's in all the murder

mysteries. I worry about you, Julie. Something weird is going on at that ranch. Three accidents in a short time. Three people who fell. At least your dad's uncle wasn't killed when he fell.

Aunt Glenda, her robe pulled around her, came into the room. I didn't want her to see Robin's last buddy note, so I quickly wrote **GTG. Bye** and signed off.

"Who are you writing to? Your mother?" Glenda asked.

I didn't give her a direct answer. "I decided to check my e-mail," I said.

Glenda sank down in a chair opposite the desk. "I can't sleep," she told me. "I knew at the time I shouldn't have had that coffee, and I was right. Millie Lee should have made decaf."

"Do you want me to make you a mug of hot milk?" I asked.

"No thanks," Glenda answered. "I'd rather just talk. Is that all right with you?"

"Sure," I said, and waited for what she had to say.

In a way, I was surprised when Glenda said, "I can't understand why there have been so many accidents." A tear rolled down the side of her nose. Almost angrily, she brushed it away with the back of one hand and said, "At least Gabe wasn't killed when he fell."

I leaned forward, hoping to get as much information as I could. "Tell me again about the first man who fell and how it happened."

"Albert Crouch? They think he was on the outside balcony of their home, which is on the edge of a ravine, and must have had a dizzy spell and lost his balance. Betty Jo saw him lying down on the rocks in the ravine when she got home from a trip to Kerrville to stock up on groceries."

"Could anyone else have been in the house with him?"

"No. Betty Jo and Albert lived alone, except for her cousin who was visiting, but she was with Betty Jo."

"Did Mr. Crouch often have dizzy spells?"

She shrugged. "Not that I know of. It was Deputy Sheriff Foster who came up with that answer. What else would have made someone fall off the balcony?"

For a moment there was real fear in her eyes. "All three falls—they *had* to have been accidents. What else could they have been?"

Trying to soothe her, I said, "If they were ruled accidents, then there's no reason for the deputy to be suspicious about any of them."

But maybe, I thought, he should be.

Chapter Eight

THE NEXT MORNING WAS SATURDAY, BUT I FIGURED THAT LAW enforcement was a seven-day-a-week business and with luck I'd find the deputy in. I asked Glenda's permission to drive into town to run errands, and she was happy to let me. The bright morning sunlight, the arrival of a new crossword puzzle magazine, and the sight of three complacent cows chewing the sprigs in her yard seemed to have eased her fears of the night before.

As I walked to the carport, Luis drove up in his pickup truck. "Hi," he said from the open window.

I walked over, smiling at him. "Are you working here today?" I asked, thinking I might change plans and hang around for a while.

"No," he said. "I'll be near here, though, and I thought I'd take the chance of seeing you, just to say hello. I'm glad I got here before you left."

"Luis," I said, desperately needing someone I could talk to, "I'm going to town to talk to the deputy sheriff."

Luis looked at me with surprise, but he didn't speak. He waited for me to explain.

I told him my suspicions and worries and that I'd talked them over with a friend online. "We both think Uncle Gabe might still be in danger," I said.

"*You* are the one who might be in danger, if this is true and you talk to the wrong people or ask the wrong questions," Luis answered. He frowned as he added, "But, Julie, remember—the men who fell were old. There was nothing to make the deputy suspect that someone had caused their falls."

"What about the missing paperweight?" I insisted.

"You didn't see it in Mrs. Barrow's house, but that doesn't mean someone used it as a weapon, then took it."

Desperately, I said, "And there are the small nail holes above the top step to the observatory."

"Which the deputy said had been put there when the steps were built."

I looked right into his eyes. "Were they?"

"No, they were not," Luis said. "Maybe you're right to turn the problem over to the deputy."

I rested a hand on his arm. "Thanks," I said.

"For what?"

"For believing me. For not saying this is all in my imagination."

He gripped my hand in his. "Tell the deputy what you told me," he said. "Then back off. Let *him* investigate, not you."

"If he will," I said. I remembered how Deputy Foster had laughed about the nail holes over the top step.

"Protect your uncle by making sure he's never alone. That's all you need to do." He glanced toward the house. "Is Mrs. Hollister with him now?"

"Yes," I said.

Luis released my hand as he said, "Just talk to the deputy, Julie. Do nothing on your own. Please?"

I nodded and backed toward the cars. I was making no promises.

About twenty minutes later, when I arrived at the outskirts of the nearest town, I stopped at a gas station and got directions to Dale Foster's branch office.

It was in a small brick building with slow-turning fans on its high ceilings, and humming air-conditioning units protruding from the lower halves of the windows. A low counter divided the working half of the room from the small entryway and the closed door marked DEPUTY SHERIFF. Behind the counter, working at a computer, sat a plump brown-haired woman whose dark purple lipstick was the wrong color for her pale skin.

"He'p you?" she asked in a low, raspy voice.

"I'd like to talk to the deputy," I told her.

"Name?"

"Julie Hollister."

"Reason?"

Her clipped questions were making me nervous. "To see the deputy? I—I'd rather tell *him*," I said.

She studied me for a long moment. Finally, she asked, "You live around here?"

"I'm visiting my great-aunt and -uncle, Mr. and Mrs. Gabe Hollister, who live in Rancho del Oro."

Her eyes flicked as though a light had flashed on inside them, and her lips tightened. "The deputy's busy," she said.

"I'll only be a minute," I told her.

"I said, he's busy."

The door to the deputy's office opened, and Foster stepped out. "Hello again. Julie, isn't it?" he said to me with a grin. "Found any more nail holes in those stairs to your uncle's observatory?"

Before I could answer, the woman said, "She's one of those Rancho del Oro people. I told her you were busy, which you are."

"Now, Myrtle, I'm not too busy to see what this young lady wants," Foster said. He waved me toward his office and took a seat behind his desk, leaning back and resting his feet on the well-polished top. As I sat across from him, I noticed that he had left the door wide open.

"So what's the problem?" he asked.

"Three men in Rancho del Oro took serious falls," I said. "Two of the men died. One of them could have. Uncle Gabe thinks someone set up something on the observatory stairs to trip him." At the smug look on the deputy's face, I said, "I know what you think, but those nail holes were smaller than all the other nail holes. Please let me finish."

He waved his hand. "Go on."

"Someone could have pushed Mr. Crouch over the balcony railing. Someone could have hit Mr. Barrow over the head with a paperweight. There *was* a heavy paperweight. Now it's missing."

Foster dropped his boots to the floor with a thump, sat up, and leaned toward me. "Far as everyone knew, no one was with Mr. Crouch when he fell, and Mrs. Crouch had a perfect alibi—she was shoppin' with her cousin and came home with a carful of groceries. Mr.

Barrow was alone, too, when he fell. Mrs. Barrow was playin' cards—lots of witnesses. Both deaths were as simple as that. No further investigation needed."

"What if they really weren't alone?" I was thinking out loud. "What if someone strong enough . . ."

He actually smirked at me. "I suppose you got someone in mind."

"Well . . . I suppose any of the men who work with the cattle on the ranch . . . or even Damien Fitch."

Foster's eyes narrowed. "How come you picked on Damien?"

"He's visited most of the homeowners, trying to sign them up for pool membership. He'd know the layout of their houses."

"His troubles with the law were all juvie. You've got no call to suspect him of any wrongdoing now."

Startled, I sat up a little straighter. Was Damien's juvenile record what Millie Lee hadn't told me?

"You haven't been payin' attention," Foster continued. "I told you, those deaths were accidents, not murders."

"But the missing paperweight . . ."

"Where are you gettin' all these wild ideas?" the deputy asked.

I slumped a little in my chair, but I answered, "I don't think they're wild. Robin and I—"

He interrupted. "Who's Robin?"

"Just a friend back in California. We keep in touch with e-mail. I've told her what's happening, and she thinks the deaths should be investigated. Robin reads tons of mystery novels. She knows how investigations should be done."

Foster stared down at the top of his desk for a moment, then raised his head and looked at me. "You live in a big city, Julie," he said. "You're used to lots of crime in and around Los Angeles. It's different out here. You just need to get used to that idea and stop overreactin'. No murders, no suspects. No crime in Rancho del Oro. Got that?"

He stood and walked to the door, waiting for me to leave. As soon as I passed him, he shut the door.

Myrtle wasn't working at her computer. Elbows on her desk, she was intent on watching me. It was clear she'd been listening and had heard every word. I just hoped she was professional enough to keep my story to herself and not consider it small-town gossip.

"You and I never did get officially introduced," Myrtle said accusingly, as though it were my fault. "I'm Myrtle Dobbs."

I nodded, trying to think of what to answer. I didn't want to say I was glad to meet her, because I wasn't.

Myrtle didn't seem to expect an answer. She asked, "What are you doing on the ranch? The people up there on the hill are all retired city people thinkin' of themselves as hardworkin' ranch owners . . . which they aren't."

I heard a bitterness in her voice and simply answered, "I'm spending the summer with my father's aunt and uncle."

She eased off a bit, but there was still a touch of suspicion in her gaze as she asked, "So you and your friend are figuring out the situation for us small-town folks?"

I blushed. "No. It's not what you think. We aren't playing detective games. My great-uncle was hurt. He insists it wasn't an accident. And because of the other two people who fell, I think there should be an investigation."

"Then leave it to the deputy," she said. "Don't start playin' detective yourself. People who don't know what they're doin' are likely to run into a lot more trouble than they can handle."

Although Myrtle's advice was close to what Luis had told me, she was not giving me a friendly warning. She was being too serious and intent for that. Why, I didn't know, but it was plain to see that she had an attitude toward the people who had bought into Rancho del Oro, and I couldn't understand that, either.

After I left the office, I drove straight back to the ranch, slowing as I crossed the bumpy bottom of the small stream. I hadn't read or answered my e-mail, and if I didn't pretty soon, Mom would be calling to find out why she hadn't heard from me.

Glenda and Gabe were involved in a two-handed gin rummy game, so I was free to go online. "You've got mail," the voice informed me.

Of course the first message was from Mom:

You aren't telling us what you're doing. I know you're probably swimming every morning, but are you helping Glenda enough? Your aunt Ellen wanted me to be sure to remind you that both Aunt Glenda and Uncle Gabe are independent people who might be too stubborn or proud to ask for your help, so you'll have to try to see what needs to be done and do it. Also, Richard read an article in some medical journal that mentioned that ginseng tea and ginkgo biloba can be disturbing to people with high blood pressure. He

wants you to be sure that Uncle Gabe isn't taking either of these. Bitsy, Trevor, and Hayden miss you and send their love.
I love you,

Mom

I clenched my teeth and wrote a response:

Everybody's fine. I'm doing whatever I can.
Love to all, Julie

What did the family expect me to do? Check the kitchen and medicine cabinet and tell Glenda and Gabe what to do? Get real.

There was a short note from Dad asking how everything was going, two ads from clothing companies, and a letter from Ellie, updating me on the swim team:

We're really going to miss you this weekend. Karen has been sick with a virus, and Laura broke a toe, so they are both out. No one's as fast as you in the backstroke, so we aren't going to place there at all. Can't wait to have you back.

Before I answered Ellie's letter, I checked the last e-mail on my list. It had a subject that intrigued me: Just for you, Julie. The screen name was PDQ, which I hadn't seen before, and all it said was

Watch for an instant message. Answer it.

Before I had a chance to wonder what was going on, I heard the familiar instant message jingle, and the box popped up.

PDQ: Hi, Julie. How do you like Texas ranch life?

Jul59: It's fine. Who are you?

PDQ: Someone who thinks you should pay attention to what your parents have told you about taking care of the Hollisters.

Jul59: How do you know what my parents have told me?

PDQ: You're in touch with Robin, too. She's a long way from Texas, isn't she?

Jul59: Do Robin and I know you? Do you live in California?

PDQ: You're not in California now. Maybe you'll wish you had stayed there.

Jul59: What are you talking about?

PDQ: You and Robin are too nosy about things that don't concern you.

Jul59: What things? What do you mean?

I waited for an answer, but one didn't come, so I sent another message.

Jul59: Hello? Are you there? Don't go away. Answer my questions.

Again there was no reply.

Jul59: I don't know who you are. Answer me.

But PDQ remained silent.

I tried to figure things out. Who knew about my computer messages with Robin? Who knew that I was living on a Texas ranch?

Glenda . . . Luis . . . Ashley . . . Deputy Dale Foster. Each of them had access to a computer.

I went back to PDQ's e-mail, clicked on **Reply**, and asked who was hiding behind that screen name and why I was being warned.

Just a few moments after I'd clicked on **Send Now**, I heard "You've got mail" and found a message from Mailer-Daemon informing me that my letter couldn't be delivered. PDQ's e-mail to me had no return address.

I needed Robin and her good advice. I saw on my buddy list that she had come online, so I told her about the messages.

Robinor: I don't know anyone who has that screen name.

Jul59: There was no return address. I tried to e-mail but my letter came back. It couldn't be delivered.

Robinor: Spammers mess up their return addresses. So do some sales companies who don't want answers.

Jul59: How can anyone do that?

Robinor: You can't if you use services like AOL or Hotmail or Yahoo. But some Internet service providers allow their members to change the "Reply To" addresses in the setup program.

Jul59: Weird! Can anyone do this?

Robinor: Anyone who knows how. Does anybody on the ranch really know computers?

Jul59: I don't know all the people here. Anyone could, I guess.

Robinor: One more thought. Who has access to your laptop? Your password is stored and entered automatically.

Jul59: No one. I mean no one except Aunt Glenda and Uncle Gabe, and I trust them.

Robinor: Don't trust anybody. In mystery novels the person who commits the crime is always the last one you'd suspect.

Jul59: Very funny. :—(If you get any more bright ideas let me know.

I signed off and leaned back in the big office chair, trying to think things through. If someone was trying to frighten me away from asking questions about the so-called accidents—two of which had led to deaths—then it meant there *was* something to investigate. Since Uncle Gabe was one of the men who had fallen, I was more sure than ever that there would be another attempt on his life.

Myrtle had told me to leave the investigation to Deputy Sheriff Foster. Luis had told me the same thing. At the moment, since I didn't have a clue what to do next, I decided to pay the deputy another visit, tell him about the warning I'd just received, and convince him he had a duty to look into Eugene Barrow's and Albert Crouch's deaths so he could protect Uncle Gabe.

After lunch, while both Glenda and Gabe were napping, I again drove to the deputy's office. Foster's door stood open so I smiled at Myrtle, walked into his office without even asking if I could, and firmly shut the door behind me so Myrtle couldn't listen in.

I perched on the chair opposite the deputy's desk and told him about the warning I'd received through an instant message.

He gave me a look of disgust and asked, "Which one of your little buddies was playin' games this time? Robin again? Or are there a bunch of you in on this Nancy Drew thing?"

"We're not playing detective. Who is PDQ? I don't know. I'm trying to protect my great-uncle."

"That's *my* job," the deputy answered. "But I seem to be havin' to protect myself from *you*." He stood up and motioned to me to leave. "I don't want you runnin' back and forth to my office anymore with foolish ideas. Be a good girl and stay with your aunt and uncle and help them like you're supposed to."

As I walked out of his office, Myrtle not only gave me a hostile look but she made a beeline for the closed door—obviously to find out what I'd told him.

I stopped on the sidewalk and took a deep breath of the clear air to help me think. I had to face the fact that I wasn't going to get the deputy's help. It was going to be up to me to find out whatever I could to protect Uncle Gabe.

Chapter Nine

AS I DROVE BACK TO THE RANCH, I TRIED TO PLAN WHAT I should do and decided the first thing was to get answers to my questions. That brought me back to Mrs. Barrow. She hadn't had time to tell me what I wanted to know about Mr. Crouch. Also, by this time, she would have missed Mr. Barrow's company paperweight—or maybe found out where she'd misplaced it. I needed to know.

At the entrance to Rancho del Oro, I eased the car over the ridges in the cattle guard and began the climb across the stream and through the hills. When I reached the Barrow house, I parked in the driveway and walked toward the front door.

As I approached the steps, a pair of familiar legs shot out in front of me. Giving a yelp, I leaped to one side, barely catching my balance.

Luis rose up on his knees and stared at me. "I didn't know you were there," he said.

"What are you doing under the bushes?" I asked.

He put down the trowel he was holding. "Digging up weeds," he said.

He was gripping something in his left hand—something metal, something shining. "What is that?" I asked.

Luis held it up. "It looks like a paperweight."

"Where was it?"

He got to his feet and handed the paperweight to me. "I saw some freshly turned earth under the bushes next to the porch steps. I poked around with the trowel and hit something hard, so I dug it up."

Dried mud was caked on the paperweight, as though it had been wet when it was buried. I scraped off some of the dirt and saw Mr. Barrow's company logo.

Mrs. Barrow walked onto her porch and leaned over the railing. "I heard voices," she said.

I handed the paperweight to Mrs. Barrow and said, "Luis found this buried under the bushes."

She took it, turning it over in her hands. "How very strange," she said. "What was it doing there?"

"Mrs. Barrow," I said bluntly. "Please don't try to clean your paperweight. I think the deputy sheriff will want to see it."

"The deputy sheriff?" Luis echoed.

"Why?" Mrs. Barrow asked. She must have answered her own question, because her mouth opened and closed as if she were a fish, gulping air. She peered again at the paperweight and said, "It is odd that this was buried. I suppose Dale Foster *would* want to know about it."

After she had walked into the house, I turned to Luis. He was frowning, obviously deep in thought. "I hope the deputy will test the paperweight for finger-prints," I said.

Luis stopped frowning and looked directly into my eyes. "Mine are on it," he said quietly. "So are yours."

For an instant I was startled, but I recovered quickly and said, "Yes, and Mrs. Barrow's and probably Millie Lee's, since she must pick it up when she dusts."

I sat on the porch steps, ready to wait however long it would take for Dale Foster to come. "And maybe the murderer's fingerprints too," I added.

Luis shrugged. "Maybe you shouldn't be so sure that Mr. Barrow was murdered."

"Someone wanted to get rid of the paperweight," I answered, "and Mr. Barrow took too much of his medication for no good reason. At least, that's what they think. The deputy hasn't tried to find out what really happened."

Luis was quiet for a moment. Then he sat beside me, so close I could feel the warmth of his body against mine. "Maybe the deputy should spend his time protecting your uncle," Luis said. "If he was meant to die and didn't . . ."

He didn't finish the sentence. He didn't need to. I shivered and clasped Luis's hand, desperately needing someone to hang on to. "I tried to talk to Deputy Foster about Uncle Gabe's fall," I confided. "He didn't believe me when I said it wasn't an accident."

Luis shifted, wrapping an arm around my shoulders to reassure me. "Do what I told you," he said. "Make sure that someone is with your uncle at all times. Don't leave him alone for a moment. I'll try to help you as much as I can."

"Thank you," I said. I liked Luis's arm around me. I liked to feel him close against me. I relaxed, leaning into his shoulder.

But then, as if I'd been slapped, I remembered. "Luis," I asked, "you know a lot about computers, don't you?"

"Yes, I do," he answered, his voice warm with confidence. "As I told you, computer science is going to be my major."

"Does that mean you know how to do things with computers that most people can't do?"

He twisted to look closely at me. "Like what?"

"Like . . . well . . . being able to send e-mails without identification."

For a long moment he studied me. Then he said, "I've heard that people can do that, but I don't know how it's done."

I was surprised. I didn't know Luis well, but from what I'd seen of him I was pretty sure he was the kind of person who would zero in on learning how to do something if he knew it was possible. Could he be PDQ? Was he trying to warn me not to ask questions?

No. He couldn't be. He had told me he didn't know how to send that kind of e-mail, and I was determined to believe him. Regardless of what Robin had said, I had to trust someone.

It didn't take long for Foster to arrive. He went into the house and talked for a while with Mrs. Barrow. Then he came out, gripping a plastic bag that held the paperweight.

"Show me where you found it, Luis," Foster said.

Luis did. They both poked their heads under the bush

by the door. When they straightened up, Foster said, "What that hole tells me is either you found a paperweight buried there, or you were buryin' it yourself when Julie got here."

"What!" Luis and I shouted almost in unison.

Foster grinned. "Just givin' you both an idea of how there are two sides to every question regarding a crime, if there even was one."

I wasn't happy with his sense of humor. Indignantly, I said, "Someone may have washed that paperweight and buried it wet. It's caked with dirt. But it could still have traces of blood on it."

He raised one eyebrow as he said, "We'll send it to the lab in San Antonio and see what they tell us. If *they* say it had blood on it, we can take it from there.

"Julie, you seem like a nice kid. I hate to mess up your dreams of single-handedly solvin' a crime, but it's not murders that's takin' place here. There's somethin' else. Everybody's figured out that there's been some pilferin' goin' on here at the ranch. Your uncle's empty Dime Box bank turned up in a flea market in San Antonio, which is how I came to know that some of the things reported missin' had been stolen."

I was surprised. "Uncle Gabe reported it stolen?"

"That he did."

"Who brought the Dime Box to the flea market?" I asked.

"Nobody knew. At least, that's what they said. That's usually the case when people don't want to be involved. Course, to give them their due, at a crowded flea market sometimes it's a quick transaction and nobody pays enough attention to be able to give a description later."

He glanced back at the house as he said, "Mrs. Barrow's also missin' her husband's gold cuff links and a diamond ring. Those are things that people could think got mislaid, not stolen, because nothin' else was taken."

"When did she miss them?" I asked.

"When? I dunno. She's not sure herself. Her husband hasn't worn cuff links for years. She just noticed they were missin' while she was puttin' up some of his things."

"What about her diamond ring?"

"It's a dinner ring she wore only once in a while. She doesn't remember when the last time was."

The deputy turned his glance on Louis as he said, "The way I see it is the thief thought he'd get a few bucks for the paperweight, but then the company logo on it scared him off. So he dropped it under the bush, dug a hole, and thought no one would ever find it. You agree, Luis?"

Luis's face reddened. "Are you asking me if I took those things?" he demanded. He held out his arms. "Search me," he said. "Go ahead. You'll find I don't have the cuff links or ring."

"No call to get riled," Foster said. "I'm just thinkin' of possibilities. The thief has to be someone who has access to the houses around here."

Indignant that the deputy was embarrassing Luis, I broke in. "How about delivery men or workmen who have jobs on the ranch?"

"That's another possibility," he answered. "Only problem is that Mrs. Barrow hasn't hired any special outside help lately. Far as I know, neither have your aunt and uncle."

Foster was being unfair to Luis. And he wasn't taking seriously my concern that the paperweight might be stained with blood. I snapped, "Maybe you aren't asking the right questions of the right people."

He gave me a steely look and said firmly, "Speakin' of asking questions—the next time you come to the office, follow the rules. Myrtle got real ticked off the last time you were there and walked right in without askin' her."

"Your door was open."

"Never mind whether my door is open or closed. You go through Myrtle."

"Who's Myrtle?" Luis asked.

"Secretary, office manager, you name it," Foster said, and, surprisingly, he chuckled. "Myrtle claims she really runs our branch office. Maybe she does, with that computer of hers. She sure won't let anyone go near it, not that anyone would want to. For all I know, she can boil eggs with it."

He began laughing at his own humor and added, "Myrtle's the smart one in her family—a whole lot smarter than any of them by a long shot. You met Damien."

Startled, I asked, "Myrtle's related to Damien?"

"He's her nephew. She stepped in when he was takin' the wrong path back in his teens and straightened him out. She's like a mother tiger where Damien's concerned."

I thought about Myrtle at her computer. I remembered my visits to the deputy's office. Myrtle had listened to my conversation with Foster on my first visit. And she'd obviously asked him what I'd said during my second visit. Maybe she was the mystery person who had sent me a warning by e-mail.

Jewelry had been stolen—maybe much more than had been reported. Two men had died. Uncle Gabe could have been killed. Why? Did any of these things connect with each other? My head hurt as I tried to fit all the pieces together.

As Foster climbed into his car and drove away, I decided the best thing I could do was stick close to Uncle Gabe, as Luis had advised me. I returned to the house.

Since Uncle Gabe was sleeping peacefully in his big recliner, I went looking for Glenda. I found her poking into the freezer.

"Oh, hi, Julie," she said, boredom slowing her words to a drawl. "I can't decide whether to bake some frozen lasagna again or steam a package of frozen low-fat chicken tamales. Which sounds better to you?"

I opened the door of the refrigerator and glanced inside. Although she usually cooked something from the freezer, her refrigerator was well stocked. "I can cook," I said. "And I've got a couple of specialties. Why don't you let me make dinner?"

Her eyes widened with surprise, and she smiled. "Really? You'll make dinner?"

She looked as though I'd told her Santa Claus had just arrived, and I felt a pang of guilt that I hadn't made the offer earlier. "I'll make do with what I can find for tonight, and tomorrow I'll drive into Kerrville and stock up on some of my favorite ingredients. Will that be okay?"

"That will be heaven," Glenda said. "You just don't know how tired I am of a lifetime of cooking."

I pulled eggs, milk, and a package of grated cheddar from the refrigerator. "We'll have dinner in a little over one hour," I told her. "It takes time for a cheese soufflé to rise."

"Cheese soufflé!" she murmured happily.

I half expected Glenda to pull up a chair and backseat-drive my journey through her kitchen, but she left me to my work, and I got busy.

By the time I called Glenda and Gabe to dinner, I had discovered the location of every kitchen appliance and tool, knew where to find the seasonings, and had made a thorough inspection of the pantry, refrigerator, and freezer. Glenda owned just about every cooking device ever invented and a nice assortment of cookbooks. Uncle Richard would be happy because there was no sign of ginseng or ginkgo biloba. Cooking here would be a snap.

The cheese soufflé was light and airy, and I served it with gingered carrots and a salad of romaine lettuce garnished with mandarin orange sections, toasted almonds, and a light vinaigrette dressing. Dessert was a medley of bite-sized pieces of apples, oranges, and pears.

Glenda savored every bite with a blissful expression on her face. Gabe ate quickly, then told me I was a good cook. "Almost as good as Glenda," he said gallantly.

Glenda blushed with pleasure, but she said, "As good as I *used* to be."

They settled into their chairs in front of the television set while I did the dishes. But I didn't join them after I'd turned on the dishwasher. The program they were watching was a rerun of a situation comedy I had never thought was funny.

I made sure that the flimsy lock on the back door was locked. I pocketed the back-door key, the key to the front door, and the key to the observatory. Then I asked Gabe, "May I visit the observatory again?"

"Of course," he said. "Anytime. You don't have to ask permission."

I didn't worry about leaving Gabe and Glenda, because I'd have a full view of the front door, but I still locked it carefully behind me as I left. I ran to the stairs that led to the observatory.

The long summer day was swiftly slipping into darkness as I climbed the stairs and opened the door. I knew my way around the room by this time, so I didn't turn on a light. I opened all the blinds, raising them to the tops of the windows, and stood back, staring in wonder at a sky filled with brilliant stars. With no city lights to dim the picture, the stars seemed to have drifted closer to earth, each one a magnificent burst of light.

I was about to adjust the telescope when a movement near the carport caught my attention. At first, I thought it might be one of the deer, come to graze, or one of the stray cattle, looking for more tender shoots on which to munch. But the movement came again, and my heart began to thud as I made out an unfamiliar outline. It wasn't an animal. It was a person.

The windows gave me a good view in every direction. I saw no sign of a car or pickup truck. I guessed that the person had arrived by horseback or on foot.

Although my legs were shaking, I left the observatory, soundlessly locking the door, and crept down the stairs. Hoping I hadn't been seen, I paused at the foot of the stairs. Then, slowly, carefully, in the meager light from a thin moon, I took a few steps toward the front of the house.

Suddenly, someone stepped directly into my path.

Chapter
Ten

I WAS TOO FRIGHTENED TO SCREAM OR YELL. ALL THAT CAME
out was a gasping, gargling noise.

The figure came closer and gripped my shoulders.
"What's the matter with you, Julie?"

"Luis?" I whispered.

"Yes, Luis," he said.

I blurted out the first thing that came to my mind.
"What are you doing here?"

"I came to see you," he said. I could hear the surprise in his voice.

"Why didn't you call me?"

"I didn't have a telephone. I worked late, cleaned
up, and ate with the men. Then I thought I'd come by
and see if you were busy."

"I didn't hear your truck."

"It's parked down the road."

"Why?" I demanded.

I felt my face grow hot with embarrassment. Why
should I have been so quick to mistrust Luis? Before he

could answer, I tried to make up for what had sounded like an interrogation. "I'm sorry, Luis," I said. "I guess I'm just jumpy."

He smiled. "Aren't you going to invite me in?"

"Not tonight," I said quickly. "It's . . . uh . . . getting late." It wasn't late. Why had I given such a dumb excuse?

Luis waited a moment before answering, then said, "Okay, then. Some other time."

Unable to think of something sensible to say, I only nodded.

Luis turned and soon disappeared into the night. A twig snapped near the carport, and I ran like a shot to the front door of the house.

I let myself in, locked the door, and hurried to the kitchen, hanging the keys on their hooks. I sank into the nearest kitchen chair, propped my elbows on the table, and rested my head in my hands, trying to sort out the thoughts that zoomed and collided inside my head.

Luis had said he had come to see me, but he hadn't driven up to the house. He hadn't rung the doorbell. If I hadn't been in the observatory, I wouldn't have known he was there.

To make everything worse, I clearly remembered Deputy Foster telling Luis that instead of digging up the paperweight, he could have been burying it. I had been angry with Foster at the time, but what if he had guessed right?

I liked Luis, and liking him confused me. I had thought of him as a friend, and suspicions were uncomfortable. "Don't trust anyone," Robin had warned.

I don't want to be suspicious of you, Luis, I said in my mind, but I can't help it.

That night I didn't get much sleep.

On Sunday morning I drove the three of us to church in Kerrville. As a big change from the casual clothes she wore at home on the ranch, Glenda had put on a smart navy-blue dress and again wore her beautiful pearls. Uncle Gabe was learning to handle his crutches pretty well, and I think he enjoyed being fussed over by some of his friends.

"Now, don't you dare tell people that you think someone tried to trip you," Glenda had warned him.

He had looked ready to argue, but before he could say a word, I'd interrupted. "That's police business—information they may not want to make public."

Gabe had pursed his lips and stared down his nose as he thought. "Yeah," he'd said. "You may be right, Julie."

"I tripped on the stairs" was all he told his friends. He didn't say how or why.

As we drove toward the supermarket where I intended to pick up a few things I needed for the dinner menu, Glenda said, "There's going to be a memorial service for Eugene tomorrow afternoon at two o'clock, since Ann will be driving to Houston on Tuesday. The funeral will be in Houston on Wednesday."

Surprised, I asked, "Have the authorities released his body?"

Gabe, who was seated next to me in the front seat, turned toward me in amazement. "What do you mean, 'released his body'? The funeral home in

111

Kerrville will transport Eugene's body to Houston. It's that simple."

I just nodded. No matter what Gabe thought, it wasn't simple. If there was any possibility that Mr. Barrow had been murdered, his body should be in the hands of a medical examiner. Robin had told me that. After we got home, I'd call Foster and ask him what was going on. Maybe he'd received the lab report. I was afraid, though, that no matter what the results were, he wouldn't tell me. As far as he was concerned, I was just a kid playing detective.

Glenda stayed in the car with Gabe while I shopped for the ingredients I needed. When we arrived home, I prepared sandwiches for lunch, eager for Dad's aunt and uncle to take their afternoon naps so I could call Foster.

To my surprise, he answered the phone instead of Myrtle.

"This is Julie Hollister," I told him. "Did you get the lab results back on the paperweight?"

"You again," he said. "Don't bug me about lab reports. The lab's always on overload. The report could take a couple of weeks."

"Then why have you allowed Mr. Barrow's body to be taken to Houston to be buried?"

"It's not up to me where somebody's buried," he said.

"If he was murdered by being hit with that paperweight, then the medical examiner should be called in," I insisted.

"You can read my report. Barrow fell. He hit his head on the fireplace and died. That's it."

"You can't be sure until you get the lab report."

He let out a long sigh. "I'm sure it was an accident, just as I'm sure you're being a pest. Knock it off. Don't bother me again. Understand?"

I didn't answer. I just hung up the phone. What kind of law enforcement officer was he, anyway?

For the rest of the day I stayed close to Gabe, uncertain whom I was protecting him from. I had no idea. Again, I wondered why the only law enforcement person around wasn't helping at all.

Late Sunday afternoon Mabel telephoned Glenda.

"The police found Mabel's gold bracelet in that same flea market in San Antonio," Glenda said as she rejoined us in the living room. "Good thing Harvey had had her name engraved inside it."

"Did the police find out who brought the bracelet to the flea market?" I asked.

"Not to my knowledge," Glenda said. She piled up pillows at one end of the sofa, then sank into them as she added, "Mabel was positively crowing and believes her ring was stolen too. She thinks it proves she isn't getting so old that she's forgetful." She shrugged. "As some of us thought.

"My amethyst bracelet must have been stolen too. I've looked everywhere and can't find it." She sighed as she added, "We've never had to lock our doors up here. We've lived here for nearly two years, and it's only lately that we've had thefts."

Mentally I went over the items that had been missing: Betty Jo Crouch's gold watch and blue topaz ring. Mabel's bracelet and ring, Glenda's amethyst bracelet, Ann Barrow's diamond ring and her husband's cuff links, Uncle Gabe's Dime Box bank filled with dimes.

Probably there were other items we hadn't heard of yet because their owners hadn't missed them.

There was no way to fix the times of the burglaries, because the owners of the stolen items didn't know when they were first missing. There was no way to connect the thefts to the deaths of Mr. Crouch and Mr. Barrow. The theft of Uncle Gabe's Dime Box had happened days after his fall on the stairs. I was totally confused. I needed to confer with Robin.

I made grilled chicken, steamed rice, and asparagus vinaigrette for dinner. Glenda and Gabe loved it. I took advantage of their TV watching to boot up my laptop and contact Robin. My buddy list informed me that she wasn't online, so I decided to write her an e-mail. As I typed in her screen name, I thought of summer Sunday afternoons in Santa Monica and groaned with jealousy. Robin would probably be at the beach. I forced myself to stop the agony. There was no way I could be in California until the summer was over. And while I was here in Texas, I had to make sure that nothing terrible happened to Uncle Gabe.

I typed in the jewelry thefts and the possible times at which they might have taken place. And I told Robin that Luis had found the paperweight. It hurt to do so, but I even told Robin about stumbling into Luis in the dark and how now I wasn't sure I trusted him.

After I clicked on Send Now, I went into the e-mail that had been sent to me. There was a letter from Mom, of course, who asked again about the ginkgo biloba and ginseng tea because I hadn't answered and Uncle Richard was still worried, and she hoped I realized that it wasn't good for Richard to worry right after having bypass surgery. Then Mom passed along Aunt Ellen's suggestion that I work out a gentle exercise program for Gabe. In the morning Ellen would send, by overnight delivery, a book from some health clinic and wanted me to be sure to set definite times each day for the exercise program and keep a record.

"Oh, right," I muttered as I clicked on **Reply**. I assured Mom that there was no ginkgo biloba or ginseng tea in the house, and that I'd suggest the exercise program and do it only if Uncle Gabe agreed.

I was about to turn off my computer when I heard the familiar jingle and the instant message box popped up.

PDQ: You're causing a lot of trouble. It's time to stop.
Jul59: I'm causing trouble? Let's talk about real trouble. Like murder.
PDQ: You're playing a dangerous game. Back off.
Jul59: It's not a game.
PDQ: I warned you to stop being nosy. You didn't pay attention. Now I'm warning you again, and this time is the last.

Another jingle, and a second instant message box popped up over the one set up by PDQ.

Robinor: Hi, Julie. We just got back from the beach. I read your e-mail, and I saw you were online.
Jul59: Robin, I'll BRB. I'm on with PDQ.

Robin immediately clicked off, but PDQ's screen had vanished, so, as I had promised, I sent Robin an instant message to tell her I was available. She came back on immediately.

> **Robinor:** What did PDQ tell you this time?
>
> **Jul59:** Second and last warning. He wants me to back off.
>
> **Robinor:** Julie, I'm scared about what's happening. PDQ could be the murderer. Maybe you should drop this whole thing.
>
> **Jul59:** That's not going to help Uncle Gabe. Whoever wanted him to fall could try again.
>
> **Robinor:** Let the deputy sheriff handle it.
>
> **Jul59:** The deputy sheriff isn't taking seriously anything I tell him.
>
> **Robinor:** Have you seen a lab report on the paperweight? Have you found out anything new?
>
> **Jul59:** No lab report yet. The lab in San Antonio is supposed to take a couple of weeks to report.
>
> **Robinor:** Julie, I've been thinking. In mystery novels, all the loose ends have to come together. Somehow the threats, the thefts, and the murders must all be connected with each other. We just have to figure out how.
>
> **Jul59:** That's what I've been trying to do. But it doesn't happen.
>
> **Robinor:** Keep thinking about it. I will too. Just remember, they have to tie together in some way. In every novel I've read they always do.

While I was getting ready to answer, Robin wrote POS and signed off. I shut down my laptop and sat there, trying so hard to think that I was giving myself a headache.

116

The telephone rang, and I automatically began to reach for it, then dropped my hands into my lap. I shouldn't answer someone else's telephone.

"Julie! It's for you!" Uncle Gabe's bellow could probably be heard down the hill.

"Thanks," I called, and picked up the phone. "Hello?" I said.

"Hi. It's me—Ashley."

"Oh, hi. Are you coming over tomorrow for a swim?"

"I wish I could, but Gran says no. Not with the memorial service and all," Ashley said. "How about Tuesday morning?"

"Tuesday will be great," I told her. I paused for a moment, then decided to come right out with what I had in mind. "Ashley," I said, "why don't you like Luis?"

Her voice dropped, and I could barely hear her. "It doesn't matter. It's a personal thing."

"I'm not trying to be nosy," I told her. "I'm just trying to figure out . . . that is, I mean . . ." I took a deep breath and said, "Last night I saw him standing by our carport in the dark. He told me he had come to see me, but he hadn't rung the doorbell, and he'd left his truck down the road. What I'm trying to tell you is that I'm confused about him. I thought that since you knew him . . ."

My words hung in the air, unanswered, until Ashley finally said, "If you don't believe Luis, then why do *you* think he was there?"

"I don't know," I said. I had no way of knowing whether Millie Lee had told her about the thefts that had been taking place on the ranch. As far as the possibility of murder was concerned, I'd confided some of what I thought to Luis and Deputy Foster, but I was reluctant to tell Ashley my suspicions—especially over the telephone.

I went back to safe ground. "I'll make something great for lunch on Tuesday," I said. "Do you like chicken salad?"

"Sure," Ashley said. "I like just about anything. Except brussels sprouts."

"Too bad," I said. "That's what we're having for dessert. That or creamed spinach."

Ashley giggled and said, "Maybe I'll bring my lunch."

"Not this time," I answered. "I promise. My chicken salad is delicious." All tension between us was gone now, and I said, "I'm glad you're coming, Ashley. It will be great to see you again."

"Thanks for inviting me," Ashley said. "I like visiting your aunt and uncle, too. They make me feel like family."

"Speaking of family," I told her, "wait until you hear what my family has decided I should do—start Uncle Gabe on an exercise program! As if he'd agree! I just wish my bossy aunts and uncles would stop telling me what to do."

Since I expected Ashley to laugh along with me, I was surprised when she said quietly, "Maybe an exercise program for Mr. Hollister would be a good idea."

"Just try to convince Uncle Gabe of that!" The silence on the phone was uncomfortable, so I tried to lighten the mood by asking, "Are you sure my aunt Ellen didn't pay you to agree with her?"

"I've got to go," Ashley said, and I heard her phone click off.

"What is the matter with her?" I asked aloud as I

placed the phone on its charger. I had hoped to have Ashley as a friend, but I couldn't figure out her changeable moods.

I walked into the living room and perched on the sofa next to Glenda. I felt a strong need to prove that Ashley was wrong and I was right.

"Aunt Ellen is sending you an exercise book," I told Gabe. "It should arrive on Tuesday. She wants me to set up a regular exercise program for you."

I waited for Gabe to explode and refuse the whole idea, but he just grunted and tucked his chin against his chest.

Glenda smiled sadly at me. "You take such good care of us, Julie," she said, "but exercise just isn't Gabe's cup of tea. Mine, either."

Guilty because of my secret delight that I'd been right and Ashley had been wrong, I couldn't meet Glenda's gaze. "Okay," I said. I jumped up and walked toward the hall to the bedrooms. Why did my family do this to me? I'd known Gabe wouldn't cooperate with any exercise program.

A short while later, as the sun was setting, I made sure that Glenda and Gabe were safely watching TV and left the house to visit the observatory. Three cows ambled into the drive, their hooves clattering on the asphalt. They stopped and watched me, curiosity on their faces.

"Go away. Shoo!" I said, once again aware that cows were a lot larger than I had imagined them.

They took a few steps toward me, and I bolted toward the stairs, reaching them and scrambling halfway up before the cows took a few more inquisitive steps in my direction.

"Go away," I said again. "Go make yogurt or ice cream or something." I unlocked the door, stepped into the observatory, and carefully locked the door behind me. I didn't think cows could climb stairs, but I felt better with a solid door between us.

The red-streaked brilliance of a Western sunset nearly took my breath away. I forced myself to remember that I was here to survey what I could see of the ranch. Red became coral and gold, then swirled under the horizon, disappearing as blackness took over. One by one, then in bursts and bunches, stars sparkled overhead. However, I hadn't come to the observatory to look for stars. I had another purpose in mind. With the observatory lights out, I watched the panorama beneath me. I saw how brightly the clubhouse was lit and remembered the posted notice for a Sunday-evening buffet.

Headlights snapped on down by the pool and a dark sedan left the parking lot. It turned up the hill to the left instead of taking the road that ran down to the entrance of the ranch. I couldn't make out the car, but it had to be Damien's. On Sunday the pool was open until nine, and it was now close to nine-thirty. I wondered where he was going.

The Crouches' house was dark. One of Glenda's friends at church had mentioned that Betty Jo Crouch had already left the ranch and her house would soon be up for sale. The furniture wouldn't be moved until she had found a place to live in Beaumont.

I could get only a glimpse of the Barrows' house, but all the rooms were lit up. Was Mrs. Barrow alone?

Were her family members with her? Did she have any doubts that her husband's death had been an accident?

Someone on horseback—probably Cal—circled the cows that had followed me, turning them back down the drive. They strolled off, Cal and his horse behind them. I watched them until they were out of sight.

Cal's appearance made me think. It wasn't just Luis whom the residents of Rancho del Oro were used to seeing around their property. Cal and his cowboys must be familiar to them too. They all had access to the homes, with those pitiful locks, and could have committed the thefts, but they wouldn't have a reason for murder—a motive, as Robin had called it. There had to be a motive, she had said.

I sat in the observatory for at least a half hour, trying to think, until I saw headlights return to the pool. The sedan parked. The office lights went on, then off a few minutes later, and the sedan drove away toward the right on the road leading out of the ranch. Where had Damien gone? I wondered. And why did he return to the pool office for such a short time? To pick up something he'd forgotten? Or to drop something off?

I let out a discouraged sigh. How could I possibly find out?

Chapter
Eleven

THE NEXT MORNING I ARRIVED AT THE POOL A FEW MINUTES before six. Mrs. McBride, Mrs. Grady, and Mrs. Templeton were already waiting for the gate to be unlocked.

After they'd greeted me, they continued the conversation I'd interrupted.

"I have no idea when I misplaced it," Mrs. Templeton said.

"Did you wear it last night to the club buffet?" Mrs. Grady asked.

"No," Mrs. Templeton said. "I decided this morning to give the ring to my daughter the next time she comes to visit. It's such a dressy ring. That's why I rarely wear it. But when I looked in my jewelry box, it was gone."

I thought about the location of the Templetons' home on the ranch. It was east of the pool, and that was the direction Damien had taken last night while Mrs. Templeton was still at the clubhouse. But she had said she didn't know when she'd misplaced the ring. It might have been missing for weeks . . . or a month. I had no right to suspect Damien of the theft simply because he'd taken a side trip in that direction before leaving the ranch.

At that moment Damien drove up, climbed out of his car, nodded at us, and unlocked the gate.

I left the chattering water-aerobics exercisers and swam short laps at the deep end of the pool. I hoped the rhythmic strokes through the chill water would clear the jumble of thoughts in my mind and help me to think straight, but they didn't. Had Damien stolen the ring? If he had, why had he returned to the pool office? To hide the ring? If Deputy Foster searched the office, would he find it?

Of course not. There was no legal reason for a search. Deputy Foster would laugh at me if I came to him with this story. I had no proof that Damien was a thief. To get proof, I would have to catch him with the ring in his possession.

I reminded myself that if Damien was the thief, he could also be the murderer. Robin had said that in mystery novels all the clues were tied together, and it was up to me to find out how these clues were connected.

On the other hand, I had to admit that Damien might be totally innocent. I was only guessing at what he might have done. Maybe Mrs. Templeton's ring had been misplaced. Or someone else had stolen it.

I climbed out of the pool, toweled myself off, and drove back to the house.

During the morning I played gin rummy with Uncle Gabe, brought him glasses of iced tea, and read to him from one of the news magazines he subscribed to. Nothing I did helped his grumpy mood. His ankle hurt and the skin under the cast itched. He was like a cross child who couldn't go out and play.

"You're not going to the memorial service," Glenda insisted. "You'll be on your feet a lot, and you'll feel miserable."

"I already feel miserable," Gabe complained.

"Then you'll make everyone else miserable," she said. "You're going to stay home and nap while Julie and I are at the service."

It suddenly occurred to me what Glenda had just said. "We can't leave him alone," I blurted out.

"Why not?" Glenda glanced at me in surprise. "He can get around on his crutches. He'll be all right for a few hours."

I can't tell her that I'm protecting Gabe, I thought. I didn't want to frighten either of them. Luis had cautioned me that someone should be with Gabe at all times, and maybe Luis had been right. Luis was still a mystery, too, but I did feel I shouldn't leave Gabe alone.

"I don't feel well myself," I answered. "Maybe it's the heat. Maybe it's something I ate. I think a nap might help me, too. Do you think the McBrides might pick you up and take you with them?"

"You should have said something earlier about feeling ill," Glenda said. "I'll call Mabel. There's no reason they can't take me. Why don't you go to bed now and rest?"

I didn't like fibbing to Glenda, but I couldn't tell her the truth. "I'll just stretch out on the sofa and read," I said.

Glenda telephoned the McBrides. Then she heated some canned chicken noodle soup for lunch, and the three of us spooned it up as if we were all starving invalids.

After Glenda left, I helped Gabe into his bedroom,

where he collapsed on top of the tightly made bed and began snoring almost immediately.

I made sure both the front and back doors were locked. Then I curled up on the sofa in the living room, where I was so comfortable in my nest of pillows that after about half an hour I stopped being an alert protector and snuggled into a half-awake, totally cozy state on the verge of snoozing.

Until I heard the back door quietly open.

I stiffened, suddenly wide awake, and held my breath.

The lock gave a tiny click as the door closed.

No one but the Hollisters belonged in this house. Whoever had come into the kitchen had no right to be here.

As quietly as I could, I climbed off the sofa. I looked around frantically for something to help me defend myself, grateful when I saw the fireplace tools. I picked up the poker, held it high, and slowly walked toward the kitchen.

I had almost reached the doorway when Millie Lee Kemp stepped through.

She gasped, and I swallowed the scream that was rising in my throat.

"What are you doing here?" we asked each other at the same time.

Millie Lee recovered before I did, but she kept an eye on the poker as she said, "You're supposed to be at the memorial service with Mrs. Hollister."

"I decided to stay home," I said, and laid the poker on a nearby table. "I didn't know who was in the house, so I—" Interrupting myself, I asked, "Why aren't you at the service?"

"There'll be plenty of folks to mourn Mr. Barrow," she answered. "There's not much else they've got to do around here. As for me, I got a schedule to keep. Mondays and Thursdays with the McBrides and Hodgeses. Hodgeses are new. I gave them the Crouches' time. Tuesdays and Fridays with the Hollisters and the Gradys, Wednesdays with the Barrows and Smiths, and every other Saturday morning with the Andersons and Templetons. I'm going to give Mrs. Nelson Mrs. Barrow's time when Mrs. Barrow leaves the ranch."

She was getting way off the track, and I had questions that needed answers. "This is Monday. Why are you here instead of at the Hodgeses'?"

"Oh, I'm goin' there in a minute. I just brought by some silver polish I was tellin' Mrs. Hollister about. Forgot it last week, and I was afraid I'd forget again if I waited till tomorrow to bring it."

"How did you get in? The door was locked."

"I have a key," Millie Lee said. "Most of the folks I clean for have given me keys. They usually don't bother to lock the doors, but in case they do I can get in without any trouble when they're not at home."

I still wasn't satisfied, and I guess she could see it in my face, because she said, "I was bein' extra quiet so I wouldn't wake Mr. Hollister. Then I thought I heard him in the livin' room, so I came in here. Only it was you, not him."

She turned and went back to the kitchen. I followed her, embarrassed by my suspicions when I saw the big jar of silver polish on the counter.

"Thanks for bringing the polish," I told her. "I'll tell Aunt Glenda you were here."

She picked up the jar and tucked it among the cleaning supplies on the top shelf of the closet. "I'll get this out of the way," she said. She smoothed down her dress and said, "See you tomorrow. You want Ashley here, too?"

"Oh, yes. Please bring Ashley," I said.

Millie Lee nodded and said, "Okay. If she wants to come."

She left, and I went back to the sofa, picking up the book I'd been reading. But there was no way I could recapture the dreamy, comfortable state I'd been in. Something was bothering me, and I couldn't put my finger on it. It was like an annoying little gnat, staying just out of swatting reach. Was it something to do with Millie Lee? I wasn't sure.

Uncle Gabe was still napping, so I opened my laptop and went online. Robin wasn't on, but she had written me an e-mail:

> We talked about motives and a list of suspects, but I forgot to tell you to find out where all your suspects were—your aunt too—at the time your uncle Gabe fell down the stairs and the time when Mr. Barrow fell and hit his head. You might be able to eliminate some of the suspects and make a stronger case for others. Talk to you tonight, if you're online.
>
> BFF, Robin

Robin really was a best friend forever. She didn't think I was nuts. She was actually helping me. I leaned back in the chair, puzzled. I hadn't asked where Glenda was when Gabe fell or who had found him lying at the foot of the stairs and called for help.

Mrs. Barrow was playing bridge at the clubhouse and had found her husband when she returned home. And Mrs. Crouch had been shopping in Kerrville when Mr. Crouch fell off their balcony into the ravine. She and her cousin had found him when they drove back to their house.

But what about Glenda?

It really wouldn't mean anything, but I decided to ask her first thing.

I went into the second and last e-mail, which was from Mom.

I hope you're taking care of your own laundry and remembering your best table manners.

"Oh, honestly!" I said aloud, totally annoyed. Mom went on.

You don't tell us anything in your e-mail letters. How are you? How are Glenda and Gabe? Send details, please. I love you. Mom

I glared at the screen. I clicked on Reply and wrote:

Everyone's fine. Details later. Love, Julie

I clicked Send Now and, after the OK, shut down my computer.

Uncle Gabe was even grouchier after his nap. Glenda arrived home and alternately fussed over him and lost her patience. Even a dinner of his favorite foods—meat loaf and baked potatoes—didn't seem to help his mood. I retreated to the observatory as soon as dinner was over and the kitchen was cleaned. I totally forgot to tell Glenda about the silver polish.

Even though clouds were beginning to drift in from the southwest, the air glowed in the golden light of the late-afternoon summer sun. Even two munching black-and-white cows at the edge of the clearing looked peacefully elegant, like cows in a children's picture book.

I swung the telescope toward the Crouches' house, which in my imagination was silently hunkered down with shade-covered eyes, setting itself apart from the active world around it.

Suddenly, a startling idea popped into my mind and I nearly dropped the telescope. Damien was my main suspect in the thefts for two reasons. One was his night-time trip in the direction of the Templetons' house. The other was his visit inside Gabe and Glenda's house, which probably meant he had visited others on the ranch and had been able to see the layout of their houses.

I had hoped to find some way for Deputy Foster to find Damien in possession of something he had stolen. Well, maybe I *could* manage it—with the help of the Crouches' empty house. I realized, though, that before I worked out a plan of action I'd have to give it careful thought. I couldn't afford to make a mistake.

The observatory was not the place in which to organize a plan. I was too distracted. I locked the observatory and was turning to walk down the stairs when I suddenly stopped.

Startled, I looked down at Cal Grant, who was waiting for me in the shadow of the carport.

"I didn't see you arrive," I told him. "I didn't hear you."

He was silent for a moment. Then he asked, "Are you comin' down or not?"

Slowly I walked down the stairs until I was standing before him.

"I came to apologize," Cal said. "Friday I was rough on you about the way you was ridin' Duffy. I had no call to be rude just because you was breakin' the rules."

"I didn't mean to break any rules," I said. "I was frightened and trying to get back to the stables."

He nodded. "Next time you take out Duffy, don't try to race him. He's an old horse so you gotta treat him gentle."

"There won't be a next time," I said. "I don't like the trails up here. They're too lonely."

"Take a buddy," he said.

His suggestion surprised me. "It would be okay?" I asked. "Do you mean I could take Ashley? Or Luis?"

"I had Ashley in mind."

I looked straight into his eyes and repeated, "Or Luis?"

"Ashley," he said.

A tall shadow separated itself from the darkness and moved toward me. It was Luis.

"Is this cowhand bothering you, Julie?" Luis asked.

I could almost feel the heat of Cal's anger, and I was embarrassed by Luis's condescending tone.

"Of course not, Luis," I told him. "Cal and I were having a private conversation."

"That must have been interesting," Luis said. "All Cal knows how to talk about is cattle."

Luis put a possessive hand on my shoulder, but I stepped away, shrugging it off.

Without another word, Cal turned and strode to the grove of mesquite that crowded the edge of the drive. For the first time, I saw Cal's horse, which had been tethered there. With one smooth movement Cal was astride, and he and the horse disappeared down the drive.

Why had Cal been so stubborn about not including Luis? I wished Luis hadn't interrupted us. I would have liked to ask Cal to explain.

Judging from Luis's attitude, maybe I didn't need any further explanation. "You'd better go too, Luis," I told him.

He gave me a beseeching smile. "Don't be angry with me, Julie."

"You were rude to Cal."

Luis gave a sniff. "He wouldn't know what being rude is. He's a cowpoke who'll herd cattle until he's too old to climb in the saddle. He'll never amount to anything."

"He chose his lifestyle. It's what he likes and wants. Respect him for it."

"Respect? He can come to me for respect when he's got a ranch of his own and a portfolio of stocks and bonds."

"Is money that important to you?" I asked.

"Of course," he said. "I guess I shouldn't expect you to understand. You've always had what you wanted. It's very different for me."

"Why are you here, Luis?" I asked. I was irritated at his answer and puzzled because he was so contemptuous of Cal.

"I came to see you, Julie. To make sure you and your uncle and aunt are safe and well."

"Thanks," I said, and took a step past him. "We are."

"Don't you want me to stay? It's going to be a beautiful evening. We could sit outside on the porch and talk."

A beautiful evening? No way. The wind had come up and it rustled through the nearby leaves like a whispering intruder. Clouds were bunching, cutting off the last shreds of western light. "I'm sorry, Luis. Not tonight," I said. "I've got a lot on my mind."

I hurried to the front door, which I quickly opened, then locked securely behind me.

I was so focused on the details of my plan to trap Damien, I found it hard to concentrate on anything else. I lost three games of Chinese checkers in a row to Gabe, after which he huffily complained that I was letting him win. To soothe him, I offered to make a cup of cocoa, but I forgot to watch the milk, which boiled over. I dropped the plate of cookies, and Glenda finally suggested that we all go to bed early.

It was a good idea, because I then had the opportunity to think out my plan to catch Damien in the act of theft. It was going to be risky, but the results would be worth it, and I wasn't afraid to put the plan into motion.

Tomorrow I'd do it. And I'd be ready.

Chapter Twelve

MILLIE LEE ARRIVED EARLY FOR HER TUESDAY SCHEDULE, bringing Ashley with her. Again Ashley carried a plastic bag with her swimsuit in it.

"Hi," she said quietly, and held up the bag. "I brought my suit, but it's cloudy. It looks like it's going to rain."

I smiled as though we were the best of friends. "But it's still hot," I said. "The water will feel great."

Glenda and Gabe greeted Ashley with what I saw was real affection. Glenda hugged Ashley, who hugged her back. I hadn't seen Millie Lee show her granddaughter any physical affection, which made me feel a little sad. Everyone likes to be hugged. Everyone needs to be loved.

A small package lay on the counter. The label was addressed to me. "What's this?" I asked.

Glenda rolled her eyes. "I imagine it's that exercise book you told us about."

I tore open the package and pulled out a slim volume.

"I'll tell Mom you and Gabe weren't interested," I said, tossing the book on the counter.

Ashley picked up the book and turned a few pages. "These are exercises designed especially for people like you and Mr. Hollister," she said to Glenda.

"We're not interested in that kind of exercise," Gabe said. "A good walk is all we need."

"Not even when the exercises will make you younger and healthier?"

Gabe chuckled. "Nobody's going to make me younger and healthier."

"Want to bet?" Ashley asked.

He looked at her sharply, but she added, "These aren't push-ups and sit-ups. These exercises are fun. C'mon. Let's give them a try. I'll be your partner, and Julie and Mrs. Hollister can be partners."

Soon we were in the living room, seated on the floor, following the exercises in the first chapter. I don't know who was laughing the hardest at the faces Gabe was making.

"Time," Ashley finally called. "That's enough for now."

As I helped Gabe to his chair, he said, "That wasn't so bad. I don't mind exercises like that."

"Good," Ashley said. "Then you can do them every day. Julie will make a chart to show what you're doing, and I'll come and help."

"You're a dear girl," Glenda said, and hugged Ashley. She quickly stretched out an arm to encircle me, too, and added, "And so is Julie."

Glenda was just being kind by including me. *I* was the great-niece. *I* was the one who should have coaxed them into doing the exercises. But I hadn't. I'd been too irritated by my family's telling me what to do. Believe me, I felt guilty and I deserved it.

Ashley had done what I should have done, and I had to be fair. "You were great," I told her as we drove to the pool. "I like the way you coaxed them into at least trying the exercises."

Ashley grinned. "It worked," she said.

When we arrived at the pool, we raced through the water until we were both exhausted. Then we lay on the webbed lounge chairs to relax and dry off. The pool was now empty, and within a few minutes Damien sauntered by, plunging his vacuum wand into the water, just as I had expected. "You kids better get in all the swimming you can now," he said, glancing up at the darkening sky. "It looks like later on today or tomorrow we're going to get a gully washer."

Kids! Did he have to keep calling us kids? I turned to Ashley, pretending to ignore Damien, and said, "I heard that Mrs. Crouch packed hardly anything when she went back to Beaumont. According to Aunt Glenda, Mrs. Crouch won't return to the ranch until her house sells. Then she'll supervise the movers, but in the meantime she's even left her valuable things behind." I paused. "I saw her little antique silver music box—a real collector's item. It's so adorable."

I had no idea what was in Mrs. Crouch's house and just made up the music box; I'd decided that an antique silver music box would probably sell well at a flea market and attract Damien's interest.

"Mmmm" was all that Ashley answered, but from the corner of my eye I could see that Damien was listening.

I was aware that I had to set a time limit so I'd know when Damien might arrive at the house to steal the box. I went on. "Glenda said something about Mrs. Crouch's son driving up tomorrow morning in his SUV to pack up the small, expensive items."

I had said all that I'd planned to say, and Damien had heard every word, so I fished around for something else to talk about. Movies? I wondered. Books?

While I was trying to decide, Ashley rose on one elbow and took a long look at me. "Maybe Mrs. Crouch doesn't think things like a music box are really important."

Startled, I answered, "They must be important. For one thing, they're very expensive. They probably also have sentimental value."

"Some people might have different ideas about what's important and what isn't," Ashley said. She rolled over, turning her head away from me.

I watched Damien slowly move farther from us as he headed with his vacuum toward the shallow end of the pool. I didn't know what was bothering Ashley, so I tried to keep things light. I chuckled and said, "You sound like you're part of my family, Ashley. Everybody in it has an opinion about nearly everything I do or say. Sometimes I get so sick of my family butting into my life."

I would have complained even more, but Ashley suddenly sat up and glared at me. "At least you *have* a family!" she snapped.

I scrambled to sit up, facing her. "Ashley, I didn't mean—"

"Maybe your mom tells you what to do because she cares about you. And your aunts and uncles do too. Have you thought of that? And have you ever thought of what it might be like if *nobody* cared what you did or where you went or even who you were?"

Shocked almost speechless, I managed to blurt out, "Ashley, I only—"

But she wasn't finished. "During the times when I'm with my mom I feel like *I'm* taking care of *her* instead of her taking care of me. And I'll probably never know who my father was. I don't think my mom even knows. And when I get dumped on Gran, she makes it clear she's only fulfilling a duty. I don't know what a real family is! You've got one, but you don't know either."

I felt as though I'd been socked in the stomach. I knew what Ashley had said was true.

But I do appreciate my family! I really do! I cried to myself. I'd let them know. I'd let Ashley know. "It's not really like that . . . ," I began.

Ashley didn't stay around to listen to what I had to say. She grabbed up her towel, stepped into her tennies, and ran from the pool. The gate slammed behind her.

I hurried after her and tried to apologize. "Forget it," she just kept saying, and she wouldn't let me drive her to Glenda and Gabe's house so she could change into her clothes. "I'll walk," she snapped, and she set off up the road.

I hadn't known I was hurting Ashley when I complained about being told what to do all the time. Every friend I knew had the same kind of complaint about her parents, and we all vented to each other. In a way, I was angry with Ashley for scolding me, but in another way I felt guilty and embarrassed and totally miserable because what she had said about me was true. I promised myself I'd try to think of some way I could make it up to her.

I didn't want to pass her on the road, so I gave her time to reach the house before I started back. I was disappointed when I found that she'd already left the house.

As I came into the kitchen, Glenda and Millie Lee looked at me questioningly.

"Did you and Ashley have a spat?" Glenda asked. "She told Millie Lee she'd meet her this afternoon at the Gradys' house. Then she ran right out the door. Her eyes looked puffy, as if she'd been crying."

"It was my fault," I said, a sick feeling in the pit of my stomach. I had wanted to make friends with Ashley, and I'd blown the whole thing. I was too cowardly to tell Glenda and Millie Lee that I'd used Ashley to try to set a trap for Damien and had then complained about my family just for something to talk about. I felt so stupid. And I had no right to tell them what Ashley had said about her own family.

However, they were both waiting to hear my explanation, so I said, "We were talking about what was really important to people and we disagreed. I said some thoughtless things that upset Ashley."

Aunt Glenda probably would have asked for more details, but Millie Lee shrugged and said, "That girl gets real moody at times. Just pay no attention, and next time you see her she'll be okay."

"I'm sorry if I hurt her feelings," I said. I really was sorry. I liked Ashley, and her blow-up *was* my fault. I wished we could start over. This time I'd make everything come out right.

"Will Ashley come back?" I asked Millie Lee. "Please tell her I want her to."

"Sure," Millie Lee said. She picked up a can of Pledge and a thick rag and headed for the living room. "She'll be over her snit in no time. I told you, for no reason I can see, that girl gets moody."

There was nothing more I could say. I went into Uncle Gabe's office to use his phone. I'd put my plan into motion. I expected Damien to arrive at the Crouches' house about 9:15 or 9:30 P.M.—as soon as it was dark. Now I'd have to make sure that Foster was on hand to catch Damien in the house.

As I called Deputy Foster's office, my hands were shaking. To my disappointment, he didn't answer. Myrtle did.

No sooner had I asked if I could please speak to Foster than Myrtle said, "He's busy right now." Then she hung up the phone.

What had Deputy Foster called Myrtle? Oh, yes, a tiger. It seemed to suit her personality.

I phoned again. "Myrtle, please listen," I said. "Deputy Foster has to be at the Crouches' house in Rancho del Oro before nine-thirty tonight. It's important. Please tell him to be there."

"I said he was busy," she grumbled, and hung up.

I sat there staring at the telephone with a scared feeling, wondering what I was going to do if the deputy didn't show up.

I turned on my laptop and went online. Robin's screen name wasn't on my buddy list, so I knew she wasn't on, but I needed her advice. Would the mystery novels she read tell what to do if a person called for law enforcement and they didn't show up?

I couldn't tell Gabe or Glenda why I needed to make a long-distance call, but I fully intended to pay for the call. I dialed Robin's number.

No one answered.

Desperately, I wrote an e-mail message to Robin, telling her about the trap I had laid for Damien. Then I told her that Myrtle had refused to let me talk to the deputy.

Tell me what to do next. You're the mystery reader.

After I closed my laptop, I told myself to forget about the plan. Let it go. Stay home with Gabe and Glenda.

That's what I'll have to do, I told myself, but I was disappointed. Damien would break into the Crouches' house to steal an antique silver music box that didn't exist, and no one would be there to see him do it.

That afternoon, after Glenda's nap, I made her a mug of tea and sat with her in the kitchen, the sun breaking through the clouds. "You've never told me who found Uncle Gabe after he fell down the stairs," I said.

Glenda closed her eyes and shuddered. "*I* found him," she said. "I drove home from having lunch with Mabel and Dorothy at the club, and as I turned into the drive, I saw Gabe sprawled on the pavement below the stairs. I was so frightened I nearly passed out!"

"You weren't at home when he fell," I said.

She gave me a desperate look. "No, I wasn't. For a

long time, I blamed myself. If I'd been here, maybe nothing would have happened to him. But I realized there would have been nothing I could have done to keep him from falling. I really wasn't to blame."

"The nail holes . . . ," I began, but Glenda shook her head.

"You heard what Deputy Foster said. They were just holes left over from building the addition to the house." She sighed. "I really don't want to hear any more about nail holes, Julie."

I put a hand over hers and patted it. "I'm sorry. I won't bring them up again," I said.

We sat quietly for a few minutes before Glenda gently pulled her hand away and cupped her fingers around her mug of tea. "This tea reminds me of the design center," she said. "The people I worked with were all tea drinkers, and occasionally we used to have an afternoon tea ceremony. It was great fun."

"You miss your interior design work, don't you?" I asked.

"Yes, I do," she said bluntly. "But Gabe was ready for retirement and insisted that buying into this ranch was an investment we couldn't miss. After a while, I stopped arguing and went along with his dream."

Afterward, I thought about what she'd said and wondered how their lives would have differed if they had chosen to follow Glenda's dream instead.

Even though I was sure that Deputy Foster hadn't received my message, I had to know if Damien would walk into the trap. At 9:15, I drove to Mrs. Crouch's house and parked down the road in a spot behind some trees where I could keep an eye on the house. Since the back of the house overlooked a ravine, I expected anyone who approached it to come from the road.

I was scared and almost wished I hadn't come. Glenda and Gabe—who was grumpier than usual—had gone to bed early. Before I left the house I'd checked my e-mail, but Robin hadn't answered.

I have no business being here, I thought. But I had to find out if Damien would come.

The clouds were scattered, so there was enough on-and-off moonlight to illuminate the drive to the house and the area between the house and the road. However, the mesquite and oaks cast deep shadows, and I jumped, clutching the steering wheel, when one of the shadows moved.

Into my line of vision sauntered four of the cattle that roamed the ranch. Someone on horseback was herding them down the hill. I leaned back, sighing with relief. No thieves. Only cows. At the moment I much preferred the cows.

I relaxed against the seat until suddenly I was spotlighted, the area around the car blasted with bright light. The light vanished as quickly as it had come, and I realized that a car had come up behind me and parked.

Before I could react, the passenger-side door of Glenda's car was flung open. Ashley leaped onto the seat, dropped a large handbag on the floor, and slammed the car door.

I stared at her, my mouth open. I was still so frightened, my heart was pounding loudly and I was unable to speak.

"The Crouches never had an antique silver music box," Ashley said. "You made that up. I've helped Gran clean their house, and I know for a fact they didn't own a music box."

"I had to make up something," I admitted.

"Why?"

"Do you know about the thefts that have been taking place on the ranch? Did your grandmother tell you?"

Ashley was quiet for a moment. Then she said, "I heard there were some thefts."

I took a deep breath and quickly told her, "I think Damien's the thief who's been taking small things from the houses on the ranch. You know . . . things that are so small their owners think they misplaced them and don't remember when they saw them last."

Ashley didn't take her gaze from my face. "Why do you blame Damien?"

"He has access to the houses here. He had coffee in the kitchen with Glenda once. She told him about Uncle Gabe's Dime Box. Later it was stolen."

"Other people are in and out of the houses here," she said. "Luis works for most of the people on the ranch—both inside and outside work."

"Are you trying to tell me that you suspect Luis?"

Ashley shook her head. "No, and I don't suspect Damien, either. I don't understand what you're trying to do."

I decided to trust Ashley. I still felt guilty about hurting her, and I wanted her as a friend. Friends are honest with each other, so I was honest and told her everything.

After I'd finished, Ashley stared straight ahead without speaking. I knew she was thinking it all over.

Finally, she said, "I think the deputy is right. No one was murdered."

"But the falls . . ."

"Gran told me that Mr. Crouch had dizzy spells. Their balcony over the ravine has a low railing. It was stupid for an elderly man who has dizzy spells to build his house that way."

"Okay," I said, "but what about Mr. Barrow and the paperweight Luis found buried under the bushes?"

She gave me a quick look. "*If* Luis found it there."

"You don't believe him?"

Ashley just shrugged, and I asked, "What do you have against Luis?"

"He's a snob," she said.

I remembered how rude Luis had been to Cal, but I felt I had to defend him. "He hasn't been snobbish with me," I said.

Ashley shrugged. "He's only interested in people who are rich. Your family has money. Right?"

I could feel my face grow hot. "Dad's a professor. Mom's an attorney, so we don't have to worry about paying the bills. But we're not what I'd call rich," I told her.

"It depends on how you look at it," she said. "If you can pay all your bills, I'd say you were rich. So would Luis. That would suit him just fine."

At the moment the last person in the world I wanted to think about was Luis. "Let's not argue anymore," I told Ashley. "I'd like for us to be friends."

Ashley gave me a long, slow look, then opened her handbag. She reached inside and pulled out a long, thin carving knife.

Chapter Thirteen

I TRIED TO SLIDE AS FAR AWAY FROM ASHLEY AS POSSIBLE, fumbling to find the latch that opened the car door. At that moment, a car swung around the curve toward us, its brights on and a row of flashing red lights across the top. It screeched to a stop in front of us, bumper to bumper, and Deputy Sheriff Foster jumped out.

"What do you girls think you're doing?" he snapped as I lowered my window.

I gulped and pointed. "Ashley has a knife," I said.

For an instant Ashley stared at me as if I were crazy. Then she said, "To protect us, Julie. You didn't think I took Gran's car and drove out here just to chat, did you? I came to protect you, just in case."

"From Damien Fitch?" Foster kept his eyes on the knife.

"From anyone who showed up on a dark road late at night," Ashley answered. She slipped the knife back into her handbag. "I would have brought Gran's gun, but she keeps it locked up."

"She has a gun?" I asked in surprise.

"Sure," Ashley said. "For when she's coming home late at night, like after she's worked at a dinner party."

I was still frightened. I didn't know whether or not I believed Ashley about protecting me, but what Foster had said startled me. I turned to him. "How do you know I've been waiting for Damien?" I asked him.

"Your friend from California phoned," he said. "Myrtle admitted she'd been hard enough on you and began to worry that somethin' bad might happen. They both gave me your messages. Now, fill me in. Tell me what you've been up to."

I told him about suspecting Damien and setting a trap for him, wanting Foster to catch him in Mrs. Crouch's house.

Foster's mouth twisted into a sarcastic smile. "Did you think Damien would come driving down the road, park in the Crouch driveway, then just walk into the house?"

"I guess I did," I said.

"By my reckonin'—let's say you're right and Damien *is* the thief—he'd park in a clearin' that's just up the road, then cut through the woods to the side of the house, climb up to the balcony, and enter the house through the French doors." He shook his head. "French doors are an invitation to burglars."

"I didn't know there was a side way to the house. I didn't know there were French doors," I tried to explain.

"There's a lot you don't know, which is why you need to be a good girl, go home, and leave investigations to people trained to do them." His voice was hard-edged. "Do you understand?"

"Yes," I said.

"You too, Ashley," Deputy Foster ordered. "Drive your gramma's car home now and stay there." He paused. "And put that butcher knife—which can be a dangerous weapon—back in her kitchen."

Ashley opened the door, but she turned to give me a pleading look before she got out of the car. "Please believe me, Julie," she said. "I brought the knife to protect us. I wouldn't do anything to hurt you."

"Okay, I believe you," I said, because there wasn't anything else I could say. But I wasn't exactly truthful. I still felt both uncomfortable and a little bit suspicious of Ashley.

"No stallin'. I'm about to let my temper go. Git!" Foster commanded.

I turned on the ignition and the car's headlights and saw, in my rearview mirror, that Ashley had done the same. I waited until she turned into the Crouch drive, backed, and headed down toward the highway. Then I drove uphill. Just at the curve, I looked back and saw Deputy Sheriff Foster's car, red emergency lights off, headed down toward the highway, following Ashley's route.

Obviously, he wasn't going to wait to see if Damien showed up. I grew more and more angry.

I thought of what Foster had said Damien might do *if* he came. There was a clearing next to the road. He'd park there. Well, so would I.

Slowly, I drove around the curve, and discovered the small clearing he had mentioned. My heart jumped as I saw a dark sedan parked to one side. Was it Damien's?

I pulled up next to it and quickly got out of my car,

wincing at the light that flashed on brightly when the car door opened. For a few minutes I stood quietly, the loud beating of my heart the only sound in my ears. I didn't dare move.

No one came, and the dark car was empty. As quietly as I could, I began to open the unlocked passenger door. The insurance card with Damien's name on it should be in the glove compartment. If so, even though I'd still have to prove my case to Foster, *I* would be sure that Damien was the thief.

There would be another burst of light when I opened his car door, but I'd have to risk it. The trees created a screen between this clearing and the house. If he was at the house now, chances were he wouldn't see the brief flashes of light.

With trembling fingers, I opened the glove compartment and pulled out a fistful of papers. As I read the name on them, I gasped with surprise. It wasn't Damien Fitch. It was Miguel Garcia—Luis Garcia's father.

A voice came from behind me. "What are you looking for?"

I let out a yelp and jumped backward, dropping the papers and banging my elbow on the car door. "Luis!" I cried out. "I didn't know it was your car."

He moved closer to pick up the papers and returned them to the glove compartment. "I told you to let Deputy Sheriff Foster do the investigating," he said. "Remember?"

Nervously, I asked, "Why are you here?"

"You were expecting Damien to come," he said.

"How did you know that?" I asked.

"Damien told me what you had said about the valuable music box left in the Crouches' house." He shook his head. "That was such an obvious setup, Julie. It never would have worked."

I was too embarrassed to think of an answer, but Luis went on. "Damien is not a thief," he said. "He's not intelligent enough to be a successful thief."

I took a step toward my own car and asked, "What do you mean by that?"

Luis smiled. "A smart, successful thief takes small things that won't be noticed, so when they are looked for, no one can remember when they were last seen. With elderly people, the plan works even better. They don't trust their own memories. They think they've mislaid or lost the objects."

"That's exactly what happened. And all the stolen things were missed during the last two months, after Damien was hired to work here." I took another step toward my car.

"Believe me, Damien is not the thief," Luis said.

Bluntly, I asked, "Why are you so sure? Do you know who the thief is?"

Luis chuckled. "No, I don't. But I'm not going to go looking for him or try to trap him. I think by now you have learned that that route can be very foolish."

I was close enough to my car to touch the door handle. I gripped it tightly, ready to throw the door open and jump inside. I was afraid I had made a terrible mistake. "Luis," I asked, "was Foster right? Were you burying that paperweight?"

For an instant, he looked at me with astonishment. "Don't you trust *anyone,* Julie?" he asked.

"I don't know why you're here," I answered.

"To protect you," he said. "It's not safe to sit alone in a car on a lonely road in the darkness of night. After Damien told me what you had said about the valuables left in the Crouches' house, he asked me if we should suggest to Foster that he keep an eye on the house. I told him I'd take care of it. I didn't tell him that it was easy for me to see the setup you had in mind."

"Damien still might have come to Mrs. Crouch's house."

"He didn't."

"You can't be sure."

"Yes, I can. Damien locked up the pool at nine o'clock and headed for home." Luis paused and looked at me searchingly. "Julie, are you sure Mrs. Crouch left a silver music box in her home? When I looked, it wasn't there."

I gasped. "You were in her house?"

"Yes. Just a short while ago, and there was no sign of the music box."

"Actually, I made it up," I said. I took a deep breath and asked, "Are you the thief, Luis?"

"What good would it do to answer no?" he asked. "Would you believe me?"

"I—I don't know," I said truthfully.

I expected him to be angry, but instead he smiled. "I heard Foster tell you and Ashley to be good girls and go home. Ashley went home. You didn't."

Before I realized what was happening, Luis gripped my arm, opened the door on the driver's side of my car, and pushed me onto the seat. "Go home, Julie," he said.

I was so rattled, it was hard for me to turn on the engine, but somehow I managed it. Automatically, I drove to Glenda and Gabe's carport and parked the car. The steps to the observatory loomed over me, and I held the bottom post for support as I gazed upward. The wide blank windows, their blinds shut now like closed eyes—when they were opened, what could they see?

It wasn't until I reached my bedroom and flopped down on the bed that I allowed myself to think about Luis.

He knew Damien wasn't the thief. But did he know who the thief was? Could Luis himself be the thief? He hadn't said he was or wasn't, and I was still confused. Would he have told me the truth if I hadn't answered honestly and told him I didn't know if I'd believe him? As I sat on the bed, hugging myself, I realized I was also just a little bit afraid of Luis. According to what Robin had told me about crimes in mystery novels, the thief should also be the murderer. Right? I didn't know the answer.

Early Wednesday morning, it began to rain, water streaking in sheets down the windowpanes, closing us snugly inside the house, away from the rest of the world. Last night's escapade seemed unreal. Ashley's kitchen knife . . . Luis's presence at the Crouches' house . . . Both Ashley and Luis had claimed they were protecting me. Why did I find it so hard to believe either of them?

I was glad it was raining. I wanted to stay with Glenda and Gabe inside the safety of the Hollister walls, pulling them around us, letting no one else inside.

After breakfast, I e-mailed Robin. I didn't know

whether or not I should thank her for calling the sheriff. She'd been trying to protect me. I wrote everything that had happened the night before, then shut down my computer without answering my own e-mail.

I spent the rest of the day playing card games with Gabe and Glenda and baking cookies. The storm passed, and a weak, pale sunlight glinted on the wet bushes and grasses. Unlike the storm, my nervous energy wouldn't go away, so after dinner I decided to clean the kitchen. While I was working, the phone rang. It wasn't my house. It wasn't my telephone. But I didn't think. I just reached for the phone, answering it.

"Julie? This is Mabel McBride," the voice said.

"Oh!" I said, suddenly aware of what I was doing. "I'll call Aunt Glenda."

"Wait just a minute," Mrs. McBride said. "First, let me ask, how are you feeling?"

"I—I'm fine," I said in surprise.

"Then you probably had one of those twenty-four-hour bugs," she rattled on. "I had told Harvey we'd be picking up both you and Glenda, so when she came out to get in the car and said you couldn't come with us because you weren't feeling well, we were sorry."

"Thank you, but I'm fine now," I said.

"That's good news," she said. "Tell your aunt that the stream's up and raging. We're cut off until all that water runs off again."

"I'll let you tell her," I said. "Hold on. I'll call her."

Glenda picked up the phone in the living room, and I went back to the kitchen and hung up. I put the finishing touches on my cleaning job. Then I opened a can of

Coke and sat at the kitchen table, trying to sort out my thoughts . . . thoughts that were making me feel creepy.

In a few moments, Glenda walked in and took a look at the kitchen. "Oh, Julie, what a nice thing to do!" she said.

I smiled at her, drank down the last slurp of soda, and walked to the pantry door to put away the cleaning supplies. I saw the jar of silver polish and pulled it down from the shelf, nearly dropping it. It was heavy. It was solid. I gripped it tightly around the neck and held it out to her. "Aunt Glenda," I said, "I forgot to tell you that Millie Lee brought this to you on Monday afternoon."

Glenda looked puzzled. "I wonder why," she said. "Millie Lee never polishes the silverware." Then she smiled and said, "Well, that was very thoughtful of her. I must remember to thank her and to ask if I can reimburse her."

"Aunt Glenda," I asked, "may I go up to the observatory for a few minutes?"

"Of course," she answered.

I pulled the key from its hook on the board, realizing again with a sick feeling that the keys to the house were accessible to anyone. I took the flashlight from its drawer. "Stay with Uncle Gabe," I said as I made sure the kitchen door was locked. "I'll be right back."

I stopped in the living room and knelt by Uncle Gabe's chair. "Were you in the observatory the day Albert Crouch died?" I asked him.

His forehead puckered in a map of wrinkles. "What day was that?" he asked.

"It was on a Wednesday," I said. I told him the date, too.

"I can't remember what I was doing that long ago," he grumbled.

"Think hard," I said. "Do you remember training your telescope on the Crouches' house?"

"I use it to look all over the area," he said slowly, as if he was trying hard to place himself in the observatory at that time. "I like to study the hills in the distance. Have you noticed that each row of hills seems more purple, the farther away they are?"

I put a hand on Gabe's arm. "Uncle Gabe, on that day do you remember seeing someone you recognized leaving the Crouches' house? Do you remember a car parked there on the drive?"

Again his forehead puckered. "No," he said. "Can't say I do." Defensively, he added, "And it's not because I'm getting old. I remember all the important things."

"Thanks," I said. I kissed the top of his head and left the house, locking the front door behind me.

The setting sun was a smear of gold, reflecting in deep reds and oranges on the clouds above it as I ran up the stairs to the observatory and opened the door. I swung it shut behind me, then hurried to raise the blinds on all the windows. I bent to aim the telescope.

I stopped, frozen in place, as suddenly all the stray thoughts in my head began to come together and make sense. Even more than that, I realized without a doubt the identity of the thief and murderer.

"I was sure you'd be up here," a voice said behind me.

Chapter Fourteen

I WHIRLED TOWARD THE DOOR, REMEMBERING NOW THAT IN my eagerness to check things out I had forgotten to lock it.

"Myrtle Dobbs," I said, my voice trembling in spite of my resolve to remain calm. "How did you get here? I heard the creek was too high for cars to cross."

"No problem," she said. "I used the department's high-ridin' big-wheel rescue vehicle."

I dared to ask, "Did Deputy Foster come with you?"

"Nope. Came by myself. To see you."

I didn't like the challenging look in her eyes as she stared at me. "I didn't expect you to come here," I said, and took a step back.

"Prob'ly not," she answered. "The people who've got enough money to buy these ranch estates aren't likely to ask workin' people like me into their homes." She glanced around and whistled. "Look at all this stuff!" she murmured.

There was only one door, one way out, which she was blocking. Wary, not knowing what Myrtle had in mind, I moved so that the center table was between us.

"I never saw a girl stir up so much trouble as you," Myrtle said, suddenly focusing all her attention on me. "You coulda got Damien into a lot of trouble. He's not a thief, you know."

"He *was*."

"When he was a kid. That don't count, and he didn't steal from the people who live here on the ranch."

"You're right. He didn't," I said, which surprised her.

She didn't ask what made me so sure or even if I *did* know the identity of the thief. She just raised her eyebrows, gave a long sigh of relief, and said, "Well, I'm glad you finally came to your senses."

She glanced around the room again, then stepped through the doorway to the small landing at the top of the stairs. "That's that, then," she said. "Thought I'd have to argue you into my way of thinkin'." She paused, staring at me intently. "Leave it up to Deputy Foster to find out who's responsible for the thefts. You're not much of a detective. You'll have to admit that."

I couldn't resist saying, "Does that mean you'll stop sending me e-mail or instant messages from PDQ?"

Myrtle gave a start. "How'd you figure out it was me?"

"It wasn't hard," I said. "You overheard all that I said about Robin and California and the rest of the things you wrote about. I had told people about my best friend, but no one else around here knew Robin's name—just you and Deputy Foster. When he told us how you could do anything on a computer, I decided you were expert enough to know how to hide your identity."

She thought a moment, then said, "Okay. No more messages, and you mind your own business and leave Damien alone. Truce." She disappeared from sight as she clumped down the stairs.

There were things I still had to prove to myself. The sky was darkening quickly, so I trained the telescope on the Crouches' house. I could see the front door and the drive clearly. If a car had been parked there, it would have been easy to read the license plate. Or if someone had come out of the front door, recognition would not have been a problem.

Gabe couldn't remember who or what he'd seen, but I knew who it had been. The person who had keys to everyone's houses and who seemed to help all and know everyone's business. I hated to believe it, but it had to be Ashley's grandmother. Millie Lee had mentioned the glint of sun on Gabe's telescope. I could picture the scene. She had caught the flash of light, looked up, and was sure that Gabe had seen her coming out of the Crouches' house. She knew he could testify to this. He hadn't spoken up right away, but he might, once he remembered, once he thought about what he had seen.

Millie Lee must have brooded about it. Each day she had become more nervous about what Gabe might say or do. So it was Millie Lee who had rigged a line across the top step to trip Gabe as he left his observatory, making sure—so she thought—that he wouldn't remember what he'd seen, put the facts together, and talk to Deputy Foster.

Millie Lee had been in the McBrides' house when Glenda had called and asked for a ride. Mrs. McBride had told her husband they'd be taking both of us. Millie Lee knew that Gabe would be home alone again.

She had an alibi because she was working for the Hodges. At least, that was what the Hodges thought.

Millie Lee had access to all the houses from which something had been taken, and she usually knew who was home and who wasn't. Could she be the one who had been stealing things? Had Mr. Crouch caught her? Had Millie Lee pushed Albert Crouch off his balcony because he'd tried to stop her? She was certainly strong enough. Robin had advised me that all the elements in the mystery had to be connected.

Robin said the murderer had a motive. I was sure that Millie Lee's original motive had been to steal for money. Then she'd had to resort to murder to keep from getting arrested.

As I straightened and took a step back, I stumbled. The room was so dark, I took a few careful steps and reached for the light switch near the door.

"Don't turn on the light," a low voice ordered.

I was startled. My heart nearly stopping, I froze as I recognized the voice. "Millie Lee?" I whispered.

"You got that right," she said, and let out a long, weary sigh.

"I didn't hear you come in."

"I didn't intend for you to hear me. I'm not stupid." She chuckled. "You made it easy, Julie. You left the door open."

"You're the thief," I said, "aren't you?"

"Thief. That's a nasty word," Millie Lee replied. "That's what Ashley called me too. This afternoon I dropped my handbag and she found your aunt's pearl ear clips and necklace. I told her to keep her trap shut because they're mine. Why shouldn't I have pearls?"

"They aren't yours. They're Glenda's," I whispered. "When did you take them?"

"Yesterday, but it don't matter."

My eyes were growing used to the darkness, and I could make her out, a tall, broad, lumpy figure standing only an arm's length away from me.

Her voice deepened as she added, "Ashley remembered seeing Glenda wearing those pearls. She put two and two together and had some crazy idea I should turn myself in. I wasn't about to. I thought she was busy scrubbin' out Mrs. Smith's bathtub, and she sneaked off and telephoned Deputy Sheriff Foster."

"The Dime Box," I said. "It was you outside that night, wasn't it?"

"So what if it was?"

My heart gave a frightened jump, and I took a step toward the door. "Where is Ashley now?" I managed to ask.

"I don't know," Millie Lee said. "She took off runnin' when I tried to stop her."

I could barely form the words. "Where are Aunt Glenda and Uncle Gabe?"

Her voice held a touch of surprise. "Why, downstairs in their house. Where else would they be?"

"You haven't . . . gone to see them?"

"Not yet. I had to see you first."

As I let out a sigh of relief, she rested a hand on Gabe's telescope. "The gleam on that thing shot me right in the eyes that day I left the Crouches' house. I knew Mr. Hollister had spotted me. I had to stop him from tellin'. I couldn't count forever on his not rememberin' what he saw and eventually figurin' things out."

I took a deep breath to steady myself, but my voice still trembled. "Does Ashley know that you murdered Mr. Crouch and Mr. Barrow? And that you tried to kill Uncle Gabe?"

"No. She only figured out what I was doin' with the pearls and probably the other stuff," Millie Lee answered. "She didn't realize I was doing it for her." She sighed again. "Why couldn't you have let well enough alone? Up until yesterday I was careful not to take things from the people I worked for on the days I was at their houses. I never came close to bein' caught, 'cept when I thought Mr. Crouch had gone shoppin' with his wife and her cousin, only he hadn't. He walked in on me goin' through his wife's jewel box. I had to do somethin', didn't I?"

"How about Mr. Barrow?" I asked. "He surprised you too, didn't he?"

"Nobody woulda thought anythin' about either of those men if it wasn't for you, Julie. You shoulda let matters alone. Nobody else asked questions, and Mrs. Barrow and Mrs. Crouch will go back to livin' the way they liked to live before. You might say I did them a favor."

Her voice dropped even lower. "What happened had to happen, and none of it was my fault. But what's goin' to happen next is your fault for deliberately gettin' in the way."

Millie Lee wasn't thinking rationally, and I didn't

know whether she would listen to what I told her. Even though my hands were sweating and I was so scared that my legs wobbled, I said, "Sooner or later you would have been caught . . . you *will* be caught. Those men had the right to live longer."

She didn't argue. She just said, "Turn around."

I didn't. I said, "You told me Ashley called Deputy Foster. He'll come. He may be here now."

She laughed. "Not with the creek high as it is. No one's comin' in or out."

"Myrtle did."

"All by her lonesome in the only vehicle they've got that can get through high water. The deputy's not goin' noplace."

"The killings have to end," I told her. "Killing me and killing Uncle Gabe won't help you."

Her low, raspy laughter was so terrifying, I had trouble breathing and had to lean against the wall for support. Her voice came out in a chilling whisper. "I'm not tryin' to help myself. It's too late for that now. What I'm after now is to get even . . . with you and with all the others. Everybody who lives up here has more than they want, more than they need. It wouldn't have hurt them none if I took a little of it."

I gave one more try. "You'll go to prison, Millie Lee."

"Stop talkin' and turn around!" she shouted at me.

Sick with fear, I knew there was no reasoning with her. I didn't answer. I didn't move. I tried to figure out what she planned to do. If I did what she ordered and turned around to leave the observatory, she'd probably run after me, pushing me down the stairs. I thought about that cement slab at the bottom of the stairs and gulped.

"Turn around!" she shouted again.

I did the only thing I could think of. I flicked on the flashlight, aimed its beam at Millie Lee's face, and turned it to high. For a brief moment she couldn't see clearly and her face was distorted with anger. She leaned forward, squinting into the light, both hands gripping a handgun.

In an instant, before she could react, I turned off the beam and threw the large flashlight at her. I heard her yelp as I dashed out the door.

She would come after me, shooting, I knew. If I ran down the stairs, I'd be an easy target. I curled into a ball on the step below the top one, trying to blend into the deep country darkness, and waited.

I didn't wait long. Millie Lee flew out of the door, heading down the steps, as I hoped she would. She didn't see me until it was too late. As she stepped out, I grabbed her ankle, pulling her off balance.

She slammed across me, facedown on the steps, and the gun flew out of her hand. It hit the carport slab and went off, the noise of the shot echoing in my head.

I held tightly to Millie Lee's ankle, but she didn't move. I knew she wasn't dead because I could hear her steady breathing. I was relieved. I had only wanted to disable her and couldn't have borne it if she'd been dead.

"Julie? Where are you?" I heard Ashley shout.

Glenda frantically called my name over and over.

"Here I am. I'm okay," I shouted.

They appeared at the foot of the stairs, wide-eyed in their flashlights' gleams. Luis appeared behind them.

Glenda gasped as she saw Millie Lee, but it was Ashley I had my eyes on. "Ashley, I'm so sorry," I said.

Ashley scrambled up the steps. She placed Millie Lee's head in her lap and brushed the hair from her eyes. "Gran! Oh, Gran!" she cried. "What did you do?"

"She must have knocked herself out when she fell, but she should come to soon. She's got a strong pulse," I told Ashley.

I looked down at Glenda and said, "Please call Deputy Foster, Aunt Glenda. Tell him to come as soon as he can."

I could see confusion in Glenda's eyes. "What shall I tell him? What happened? Who tried to shoot you?"

There was no point in trying to hide the news from Ashley or Glenda. I took a deep breath. "Millie Lee was the thief. Then she killed Mr. Crouch and Mr. Barrow because they caught her stealing their wives' jewelry. She even tried to kill Uncle Gabe because she thought he had seen her leaving the Crouches' house. A few minutes ago, she tried to get rid of me."

Ashley stared, her face turning pale, her lips parted as though she wanted to speak but couldn't.

"Oh, Julie!" Glenda said. "My goodness, you've been in such danger." She took a step toward me.

"I'll be okay," I said.

"Ashley," she said, "is this why you came to us? You didn't tell us why you were so upset."

"Please hurry, Aunt Glenda," I told her. "Call the deputy and an ambulance."

As Glenda turned and began to hurry toward the house, Millie Lee gave a little moan and began to stir. I tightened my grip on her ankle.

Ashley sat up and looked at me, and I could see the tears spilling down her face.

"I'm sorry, Ashley," I said again.

Luis stared up at us. "Julie," he said, "tell me what I can do to help."

"Why are you here?" I asked him.

"I've been trying to protect you, of course. You haven't realized that I have been faithfully at your side," Luis answered.

Maybe it was the pompous tone in his voice that set me off. "You're kidding," I said without thinking. Then, quickly, because of the hurt expression on his face, I added, "Come up here on the steps, Luis. I'll tell you and Ashley everything."

Glenda returned, the beam from her flashlight wobbling as she hurried. Carefully, she climbed the steps and sat with us. "I told Deputy Foster what Julie said. He's got access to a helicopter. He can land on the ranch's airstrip, and he'll be here in a few minutes."

She reached for Ashley's right hand and held it tightly. "I also spoke with him about Child Protective Services. If it's all right with you, Ashley, Gabe and I could become your foster parents. The sheriff said he could make the recommendation. There shouldn't be any trouble since you'll need a new home."

Ashley burst into sobs, but she kept saying over and over, "Thank you. Yes."

Glenda looked at me and said, "Julie, you are a special girl and I don't know what this family would do without you. Wait until the relatives hear about all this."

I smiled, then turned to Ashley. She was my friend—practically family now—and she was hurting.

Later I'd tell them what had taken place in the observatory. And I could envision telling the same story over and over.

First, I'd tell it all to Robin. Because she was my best friend. I wouldn't point out to her that she merely read murder mysteries and I had actually solved one. The rest of the summer was still a mystery to me, but I was no longer worried about how it would turn out.